WE

BOOK ONE IN
THE GAMES TRILOGY

WILL

GENEVIEVE JASPER

RULE

Copyright © 2022 Genevieve Jasper

All rights reserved.

The characters and events portrayed in this book are fictitious. Any similarity to real persons, living or dead, is coincidental and not intended by the author.

No part of this book may be reproduced, or stored in a retrieval system, or transmitted in any form or by any means, electronic, mechanical, photocopying, recording, or otherwise, without express written permission of the publisher.

Cover Designer: The Pretty Little Design Co.
Editor/Proofreader: R. A. Wright Editing
Formatter: R. A. Wright Editing

Chapter 1

Harlow

It's times like these, when a random man lays on top of me flapping about like a salmon, that I really question my life choices. I should just kick him out right now. His clammy flesh is so flush with mine that I can't even snake a hand in between us to play with my clit. But my mama didn't raise a quitter. Well, my mama raised no one, but you get the gist. Instead, I push on his shoulder in the universal sign for position change and straddle him when he lays on his back. God, he's not even that good looking now I'm sobering up. I avoid his eyeline awkwardly. Why did I go home with him again? Oh, yeah. It's a Tuesday, so slim pickings out of the already small bunch of prospects at the bar I frequent to avoid the Guards.

Why bother trying on a Tuesday if I know this is the standard I get? you might ask. I'm not hideous, I promise. Just kind of desperate. And yes, I know that's probably worse. Sawyer had a date tonight, and by date, he means a session with a fuck buddy, so I need one too. It's common sense. There's nothing more pathetic than having to sit alone in my room, listening to him and whatever random girl he's chosen for the night having a great time while it's just me and a toy. I won't do it. Not so soon, anyway.

Focus, Harlow. Cole? Cain? Colin! Colin looks up at me like he's having the time of his absolute life, while I try not to sigh dejectedly when I come flush with his lap and there's a lot less inside of me than I was hoping. You really should be able to check these things out before you commit to bringing guys home. By the time you realize they're lacking in that department, it's more effort to kick them out and sort yourself out. I do the best I can when Colin doesn't even meet my thrusts, changing the angle myself by leaning back and finally getting to my clit.

"You look like a fucking Porno Barbie," he breathes, clearly in awe, but it pushes the beginnings of an orgasm away. I really wish he wouldn't speak. I hate that comparison.

Closing my eyes so I can picture someone else, the sounds from next door pick up again at the perfect time, helping me build my release. I try not to focus too hard on who I'm picturing, because now is not the time to be judging myself. I roll my hips, leaning back on one hand so Colin drags against my front wall as I twirl my fingers around my clit, imagining the sounds from next door are being whispered into my ear rather than eavesdropped through a wall, and I'm so close. That is, until Colin gurgles like he's drowning on his own spit, jerks around like he's been electrocuted, and pulses into the condom before going limp instantly. Fucking hell. What is my life? He goes to hug me as I roll off him, but I keep rolling, stand up, and throw a T-shirt on.

"I've got a really early shift," I lie, attempting to look apologetic before glancing obviously at the door. I should feel bad, but after that poor performance, I really don't. I head out of my bedroom and to the bathroom before he can mutter anything. Finally, my luck is turning—he's out of my bedroom fully dressed and ready to go when I'm finished.

"I had a great time," he says as we convene in the kitchen by the front door. I smile and nod. Not that I have any issues with lying, but he doesn't deserve the effort. Sawyer comes out of his room next to mine and heads into the bathroom. Colin goes to kiss me while he thinks I'm distracted, but I step back, opening the door instead.

"See you later," I say as I shut the door behind him and head to the coffee pot. Caressing it with one hand, I try to decide whether I should get a few hours of sleep in now or start shotting caffeine straight away. As I'm deciding, Sawyer joins me in the kitchen area.

"Jesus, how old was that one, Harlow?" He sounds aggravated considering I just heard him come, but I shrug—because I genuinely don't know or care—and turn to face my best friend in the world.

If I'm Barbie, Sawyer's my Ken. Plenty of people have called us that over the years since we met as kids. That's probably why when we were surly teenagers who got the ick from the opposite sex, we made a pact to never be together. For whatever reason, it hasn't changed . . . although he definitely has. Gone is the shy pale-haired choir boy from our childhood.

Sawyer slowly but surely turned into sex on legs. His dirty-blond hair, slightly longer on top, highlights his bright blue eyes, and his solid jaw that's always dusted with stubble has helped get rid of the "innocent" look. The defined muscles from his job at the gym and natural tan have done the rest. Sawyer is hot, and he's quickly becoming my go-to fantasy when reality doesn't cut it, which happens to be *all the damn time.* I really need to nip that in the bud. He steps forward, hugs me, and presses a gentle kiss to my hair before murmuring, "What are your plans for the day, Angel?"

"I've got work at ten." My reply is muffled, my cheek pressed up against his impressive pecs. "What's the time?"

"Five. You with *Nico* today?" he asks, tickling my ribs lightly. My cheeks heat even though he can't actually see me, which is embarrassing.

"Shut up." I am, and I'm already excited enough, which is ridiculous seeing as I see him multiple days a week. I don't bother to reply any further. "Coffee or sleep, then, I guess." He chuckles, and my whole body shakes with his laugh, warm in his embrace.

"How about sleep, then coffee? I'll get rid of . . ."

Now it's my turn to chuckle. "Chivalrous as ever, Sawyer."

"Whatever. I'll get rid of her, then we can take a nap. Go have a shower. You smell like dick." With that charming observation, he lets me go and walks back to his room. I wait for his *friend* to use the bathroom before I hog it for a shower—because I'm a great host—but it only earns me a glare as she walks back to his room, so I wish I hadn't bothered.

I hear the front door shut while I'm scrubbing myself clean, and then the bathroom one opens. I poke my head around the shower curtain and see Sawyer grabbing linens out of the cupboard. He's turned away from me, and I'm slightly distracted by the way the muscles bunch and contract in his back, his tan skin calling to be touched. I feel a zap of energy through my body that ends up pulsing between my legs. Chastising myself, I dip back behind the curtain before he can catch me ogling him. The pact, Harlow! But I'm not propositioning him, just enjoying the view. How can a woman live with someone who looks like Sawyer and not develop a teeny-tiny crush? Mine has definitely been developing since we moved in together. Plus,

I didn't get to finish—that's my excuse for acting like a horny teenager.

I finish up in the shower, climb out, and roughly dry my hair before walking back to my room in my towel. When I get there, I notice my bed is made with fresh sheets and the window is open, airing out any lingering Colin smells. Sawyer is seriously the best. I dress in some sweats and a crop top—my favorite lounging outfit—and meet him in the living room, joining him on the overstuffed corner couch. We've lived here just over two years now and haven't changed much, but we recently splurged on this couch, and it's the best decision we ever made. It sits with its back to the kitchen area that opens up straight from the door. The bathroom is on one side of the large open plan space, and our bedrooms are side by side, opposite the bathroom and laundry. Storage space is an issue, but we make do.

Sawyer lifts the blanket he's under without breaking his gaze from the TV, and I happily take up the role of little spoon. This is another reason I would never risk the pact. Sawyer makes no indications that he's interested in me as anything other than a little sister. He looks after me, makes sure I eat, strokes my hair so I sleep—like he's doing now, to my delight—and he touches me a lot, but never in *that* way. It's intimate, but clearly not sexual for him. And it didn't used to be for me, but slowly, over the last two years, it's developed. However, even pressed up against him now, he's distracted by the TV. As I lay enveloped in him, I promise myself I won't be taking any more sneaky looks at his muscles or getting off to the sounds of him with another woman. What we have is way too perfect to ruin with my libido.

I sleep like the dead, as I always do in Sawyer's arms, and wake up when he gently shakes me. "Time to get up, Angel."

Rolling onto my back and stretching out like a cat, I rub at my eyes with my knuckles.

"What time is it?"

"Nine-thirty. I'll get you some coffee." He's already up and walking behind the sofa to the kitchen area by the time I open my eyes, so I sit up to watch him. No, Harlow! Have some restraint. I go into my bedroom and get dressed for work, putting on some soft black jeans and a long-sleeved top, and slide my phone into my pocket. We can wear what we want under our aprons, but black is easy and hides any spills. Sawyer has disappeared when I come back out into the living area, but I spot a steaming thermos of coffee on the counter and practically pounce on it. The few hours of sleep worked wonders, but coffee will always be needed. I take a long sip, ignoring the burn, and moan at the delicious liquid. Spinning round to lean against the counter, I jump slightly when I see Sawyer standing still, watching me with his own coffee in hand, dressed for the day too. Why is he looking at me like that?

"Surely you just burned every taste bud off?" he asks as he blinks a few times, joining me in the kitchen. Oh. I shrug, trying to tamp down the disappointment that his look didn't mean anything more. Honestly, this crush is getting out of hand. It's because I have to see him half-naked all of the time and listen to his bedroom activities, that's all. Hence why I normally go out and get my own one-night stand when he does, but I need some better specimens than Colin if that's going to carry on working. "Are you ready?"

"Let me brush my teeth." Once my teeth and hair are brushed, the latter thrown up into a bun, Sawyer is waiting at the door and hands me my thermos back. I grab my keys and wallet off the island on my way past and slide on my Vans, passing Sawyer as he opens the door for me. As he turns his back to me to lock up, I take one last look. I won't see him for a while now, so why not? Wearing gym shorts, a hoodie, and a backward baseball cap, you could assume why his classes are so popular. It's not just that, though—he also cares about his clients and is really good at his job. I should know. He tutors me privately for fitness and defense, and I've never been stronger.

As we start down the stairs, our landlord is coming up them. We don't see her often, but she's lovely and obviously has a soft spot for Sawyer, as most women do. He got the lease to this place on his own when he turned eighteen, so I technically sublet a room from him.

"Hi, Sylvie," Sawyer says as we stop. "I didn't know you were coming. We're heading to work."

"Hi, Sawyer, Harlow. That's okay, I'm here to make sure 2b is empty." I didn't even realize they'd moved out. We barely see our hallway neighbors anyway. "It will have new tenants next week."

"Oh, great. Okay. See you later." We all smile, and Sawyer and I carry on down the stairs and out the front door. The coffee shop I work at is only a ten-minute walk away, and then Sawyer's gym is five on from that. He picked a great location for our apartment and somehow got a great price to lease it for, but I'm not surprised—he's a charismatic miracle worker. He's quiet on the walk over, which isn't unusual. He's not a massive morning person at the best of times, and the sleep we got this morning isn't a decent amount for a normal person. It was great for me—I can't seem to sleep well alone, so I don't sleep a huge amount anyway—but I'm sure Sawyer is feeling it.

"Do you want to skip training tonight?" I ask, and he turns his head to look down at me.

"No, I'm good, Angel."

I love when he calls me that. It started when we were young and has been his nickname for me ever since, long after he realized it wasn't true.

"Are you sure? You look dead on your feet," I say.

"It's important to stay regular. You need to be ready."

"Sawyer, we have three years."

"Not just for that. We both know the Guards are getting worse. I want you to be prepared to handle anything."

I scoff. "If the Guards try something, we both know there's no fighting back." He stops still and grabs my arm to turn me to look at him.

"If they ever try anything, that's exactly what I want you to do. Whatever it takes to get to safety. We'll figure out the rest once you're back with me." He looks so serious, I nod. "Promise me, Angel. Just get back to me."

"I'll always try," I promise. That seems to satisfy him, because he starts walking again.

"So, training just after six?"

"Seven thirty. I've got a session with Nico tonight." He doesn't say anything, but his jaw tenses, and I suddenly feel guilty. "Sorry, don't wait around for me. We'll reschedule." He wraps his arms around me as we stop in front of the coffee shop, squeezing me hard before dropping a kiss on my hair, then pulling back.

"I'll see you at seven thirty at the gym. Get Nico to walk you, it'll be dark by then."

"Okay." He turns and walks away, and I watch him like a lovesick puppy.

Chapter 2

Harlow

Pushing through the glass door of The Grind, I see Fleur smirking at me from behind the counter against the far wall.

"I need to get laid," I grumble when I've joined her behind the counter, and she laughs.

"To stop you perving over Sawyer? The guy from last night no good?" It was Fleur, my other best friend, who I'd been out with last night. We met at this job when we both started as soon as it opened. We'd just turned eighteen, and she was the perfect partner to work, gossip, and party with. She still is.

"No good at all," I confirm as I head through to the back to put my stuff in a locker. I pop my apron over my head and tie the back as I rejoin her. "How's it been?" I ask. It's not busy right now, which is unusual for midmorning.

"Pretty quiet, honestly. We'll see how lunch is."

"Where's Nico?" I know he's on the split shift today, covering the first and last four hours, so he should be here for me to take over.

"He left a little early. Had an errand to run before class." I mock myself internally for the disappointment I feel. *He'll be back this afternoon when Fleur leaves. Don't be so ridiculous, Harlow.* The bell rings then, and as karma for the relaxed morning, the lunch rush is mayhem. That'll teach us for using the *q* word so freely. It's a curse to say "quiet" in hospitality, and Fleur should have known better.

Before I even get to have a cup of coffee myself, Nico is walking back through the doors, his tall, lean frame squeezing around chairs and between customers. The time has flown by, so I'm not expecting him, and I nearly scald myself when I get distracted from the white hot chocolate I'm pouring as I attempt to watch him make his way over to us. I see him around four out of seven days a week, and it's still not enough to get used to him. His hair is a cool dark brown with a slight wave. It could probably be tied back in a few weeks, but for now, it's permanently being pushed back from his face and curls around his ears, just meeting the short beard he keeps. Every time it falls into his face, I want to stretch up on my tiptoes and run my hands through it. It looks so soft. God, he's gorgeous, and I crush on him so hard.

I wrench my attention back to the customer and hand over their drink. Fleur gives my arm a squeeze a few minutes later as she leaves, and Nico picks up where she left off. My body is always aware of where he is as he flits around, making different drinks and bites to eat as I take orders. It finally calms down about an hour later, and I clear some tables while he sorts out the catastrophe that is the coffee machine. I load the dishwasher out the back and bring a clean rack of cups out with me, which he takes as I come through. It takes a decent amount of effort to not get distracted by the flex of his biceps as he maneuvers the rack onto the side. Nico isn't as built as Sawyer, but every peek I get suggests he's not shy of definition.

"Thank you. And hi," I say with a sigh, happy for it to ease up a bit for now, although we sometimes get a rush before closing as people finish work.

"Hi," he replies with a shy smile that makes my knees weak. "How have you been?" We haven't crossed paths in a couple of days, and it feels like ages since I've seen him.

"Not bad, you?"

"All good. Busy." Nico is studying criminology in between his shifts here, and he's brilliant. He's also teaching me everything there is to know about the previous Games tasks, although he doesn't explicitly know that. I wasn't the most academically gifted at school—even though I'm reasonably intelligent in general—and yet he's managed to explain everything I've asked of him well enough that I understand and can relay it to Sawyer. He's the most attractive geek I've ever met—a perfect mix of insane intelligence and shy hotness. I'm such a fangirl, it's embarrassing. Unfortunately for me, Nico is out of bounds because we work together, and he doesn't seem interested anyway. So, of course, I'm obsessed.

It's a sick joke. I have no trouble whatsoever finding guys to take home thanks to the "Barbie" resemblance, but the two guys I actually like want nothing to do with me. Maybe that says something about my personality? Or maybe it's a case of me wanting what I can't have. Throughout this depressing inner monologue, I realize I'm staring at him, so I clear my throat and look away.

"Are we still okay for tonight?" I ask. I do feel bad for taking more of his time when I know how busy he is, but the sessions are invaluable, and honestly, I can't make myself stop having that extra time with him with no distractions.

"Of course," he says. "Here?"

I nod as a customer comes through, and we're steadily busy for the remaining time we're open, cleaning up around the final patrons so we can finish as quickly after we close as possible. This place isn't exactly my dream job, but it's flexible and I work with great people, so it's perfect for now. Plus . . . free coffee.

I flop down into my seat with a groan and place my head on my forearms just for a second, closing my eyes.

"Late night?" Nico asks. Colin flashes through my mind, and I cringe at the idea of Nico finding out how little I settle for in my hookups.

"Yeah. That'll teach me for going out on a school night," I joke as I lift my head. He's sitting in the chair perpendicular to me, as always, and I get a look at him up close. Did I mention that Nico is gorgeous? His eyes are dark like his hair, and he has long sooty lashes that frame them perfectly. He's got his glasses on now, which would probably convince me to complete these study sessions even if I no longer needed them. I swear I go into a trance sometimes and don't realize I'm staring for an embarrassingly long time, but this time, he's staring back. He tucks some stray hair behind my ear, and I stop breathing, but he gives me a concerned look and drops his hand as soon as the hair is secure. Is that friendly? Flirty? I second-guess everything with him. How am I so secure and confident with everyone except him? And Sawyer, when it comes to my crush.

"You sure you're okay for this?" he asks.

"Why? Wanna blow it off and go get huge burgers instead?" His eyes widen slightly, and I realize that it must seem like I'm asking him out. Before I can freak out and trip over myself to explain, he's looking back down at the work.

"If you can power through, we can get through this session as quickly as possible. It's not a meaty one."

I open my mouth, but nothing comes out straight away. Did he just shut me down and say he wants this over as quickly as possible all in one? *Ouch.*

"Of course," I get out eventually. I think about offering to just end them, but honestly, I don't want to. Even if I make myself look like a fool more often than not, he's such a great teacher, and I need to know this at a minimum. He teaches me so much more than I've been able to find out for myself. Also, I'm selfish. I love the time we spend together, even if he doesn't.

An hour flies past, and I manage to swallow my dented pride and focus, forgetting it altogether as soon as Nico starts explaining the lesson. It's super interesting, and I already can't wait to relay it all to Sawyer. You can find some details of previous Games online, but what happens behind closed doors mainly stays behind closed doors. Nico's course seems to go into a lot more detail, which is lucky considering the information isn't broadcast anywhere. Information about The Games has been kept under lock and key since its conception.

It's a quarter past seven by the time we're finishing up. Nico stretches and his shirt lifts, showing a stretch of skin and a hint of abs. Before I can do anything ridiculous like lick them, I force my eyes away and stand to wash and put away our mugs.

"What are your plans for the rest of the evening?" Nico asks behind me.

"I'm hitting the gym."

"With Sawyer?"

"Yep." I talk about Sawyer enough that Nico would know who he was, even if Sawyer didn't frequent the coffee shop.

"I'll drop you there."

"Thanks," I say gratefully. It's not far, but it's dark out now, and you can never be too careful. The Guards don't tend to come this far out, but it's not impossible. We lock up and head toward Nico's car to head to the gym. The silence isn't awkward—things are only awkward with us when I put my foot in it. We're both tired and enjoying the peaceful drive after a busy day.

"What are *your* plans for the evening?" I ask Nico when we're nearly there.

"Honestly, I'll probably faceplant my bed."

"I hope I'm not keeping you from anything or anyone else with these study sessions," I offer, only half digging for information.

"If I didn't want to do them, I wouldn't," Nico replies, but when I look up, he looks pensive. I wonder if that's actually true, but I think it is. Even if only for the fact he loves to geek out and share his passion for what he's learning with someone else.

"Okay," I concede. We turn the corner and see the glass-fronted Urban Fitness right up ahead. The whole place looks so modern. This area really will become so popular in the near future, which is a worry. Will gentrification bring the Guards, or will we be priced out of the area first?

"I should switch my membership, you know," he muses as we pull up outside.

"You say that every time you see it," I remind him.

"And I mean it. Maybe we could work out together." Nico never initiates us doing anything together beyond studying. I try not to either, as I'm sticking to the rule of not fucking where you work. I do slip up sometimes, hence the burger offer earlier, and I'm sadly buoyed by Nico's suggestion.

"Why don't you come in now? They offer trial sessions if someone introduces you."

"I don't think I could stand for long enough to *watch* a session, let alone actually train. Rain check?" he says.

"It's a date. I mean, not a *date* date. It's a figure of speech." Jesus, why do I turn into a bumbling idiot when I'm around him? Nico smiles tightly.

"I know, Harlow. Don't give yourself an aneurysm. I'll see you tomorrow." I take that as my dismissal, and he watches me walk in before leaving as I cringe at how ditzy I am with him. He must think I'm a fool. Where's super-hot, sexy Porno Barbie when you need her?

Chapter 3

Sawyer

I'M IN THE BREAK room, trying not to fall asleep into my drink, when Taylor pokes her head round the door.

"Your girl's here, Sawyer." I don't bother to correct her. It won't stop her from saying it, and I kind of like hearing it. Draining the water, I put the glass into the dishwasher and wander out to the main gym. Taylor is back behind the desk and nods toward the locker rooms. "She's gone to get changed."

"Okay, thanks." I make my way into the gym, and even though it's quietened down a bit since the after-work rush, there's still a decent crowd here. Thankfully, there are two free treadmills next to each other, so I program them both and start walking on mine while waiting for Harlow.

I see her appear in the entryway before she sees me, and I watch her scan the floor. She's got the resting bitch face on, which I'm thankful for because she looks incredible, her icy-blond hair in a bun that lets her face show off its natural beauty. She always looks flawless and gets an unlimited amount of attention, but guys especially can't help themselves when she's in Lycra, and I don't blame them. I can barely help myself. The resting bitch face doesn't deter many men, but any deterrence is a good thing in my book. I watch her until her gaze settles on me and her face brightens, dropping the act and letting those plump lips split into a smile as she makes her way over. I would do many, many things to keep earning that smile.

"Hey," she greets me. "How was your day?"

"It felt long," I admit. We both have way longer days than this sometimes, but the late-night partying was not a good idea. Am I getting old at the ripe age of twenty-one? "How was yours?"

"Same. I can't wait to get home."

"Via Chung's?"

"Eurgh, you're the best," she groans. She says that so much it's her default response, but I love it every time.

"You won't be saying that in half an hour. We're doing cardio today."

"I would never moan about what you think I need," Harlow replies in an innocent voice, but we both know that's bullshit. Which is exactly why I sweetened her up with the promise of Chinese food in the first place.

"Ha, okay."

"Not to your face, anyway."

"At least it's a short one," I offer. Cardio is her least favorite form of training, but it's also necessary. I don't train her so hard to lose weight—Harlow is already perfection. It's her strength, her self-defense skills, and her stamina that I want to also be in peak condition, and they're getting pretty close. She works hard while she's here, and I push her to her limits. The added incentive to this is if I'm more focused on burning muscles and teaching new skills, then I'm less focused on how much of Harlow I can see.

"That just means it's full of inclines and speed," she says with narrowed eyes in my direction. Miming zipping my mouth shut, I lean over and press start on the programming of her machine.

Half an hour later, she flops from the treadmill and lies on the ground, chest heaving with every breath. I know if I managed to tear my gaze away, I'd see every man in our vicinity looking at the same thing.

"Oh my god, you're a sadist," she pants.

I chuckle as I throw a towel at her. It lands perfectly over her chest and face, hiding the show from everyone, but she doesn't move it. I wipe my own face and the machines down, and she's still down there, so I crouch to peel the towel away from her eyes.

"Are you dead?"

"Probably."

Standing back up, I hold my hand out, and she takes it. She puts her other hand on my arm to steady herself as I haul her up. My hands itch to pull her into my arms, and she probably wouldn't even think that was weird for us, but I need to rein myself in. I thought touching Harlow innocently whenever I wanted would help take the edge off this craving I have for her, but it's not working out that way at all. If anything, it's making it worse, pushing me to take it further. Maybe I need to wean myself off her. Waiting for her to stabilize, I take a step back so her hand drops, and I gesture to the lockers.

"Come on. Chow mein waits for no one."

Chung's is right across the road from our apartment, so I watch Harlow go home and then go in to order. A call comes from behind the counter as the bell rings.

"Hey, Sawyer."

"Hey, Chung."

"The usual for you and Harlow?"

"Yes, please."

"Where is she?" he asks, looking around me as if I might be hiding her, but he's out of luck tonight.

"She's gone home."

"Good. It's not safe for women out so late. Not safe for anyone, really."

"Don't I know it."

I scroll mindlessly on social media while the food's prepared and then carry it home, leaving it on the kitchen island while I take a shower. Harlow left out clean sweats for me on the bathroom counter, and I smile. We're like an old married couple already. I love it. Registering that she was naked in here minutes before, the steam still in the air from her shower, has me feeling a certain kind of way. *Don't do it, Sawyer.* I tell myself it's pervy to jerk off over my best friend when she has no idea, but knowing it and being able to stop it is one thing, and it only works half the time. Trying to get the image of her wet curves out of my head, the image of her heaving chest covered by a sheen of sweat pops in instead. Not helpful in the slightest. I run through the alphabet listing gym equipment to keep my mind distracted and climb out, drying and dressing quickly. By the time I'm back out, Harlow has dished up and is pouring out drinks.

"Thanks, Angel," I say as I take a seat.

"Want me to explain what I learned while we eat so we can crash after? I'm on early tomorrow." She grimaces. I nod around a mouthful of noodles, and she talks me through what she covered with Nico today. Her face brightens when she mentions him, just like it did in the gym earlier with me, and my mood sours. I don't know what Nico's problem is, and I haven't asked, but every time I go into the coffee shop when they're both there, I catch him watching her. And there's no way you can spend that much time with Harlow and not fall for her personality, even if for some strange reason you didn't find her attractive.

It can't be long until he makes a move, no matter how shy he seems, and watching Harlow with a boyfriend will be so much harder than seeing her with all the random losers she uses for a night. Or would it help? A tangible reason to calm down with the touching and napping and couple activities? I know Harlow says she doesn't want to get into anything with someone she works with, but I know she'd break that rule for Nico if he ever got around to it. Or maybe he has the same rule? Maybe he doesn't want to risk having to work with someone who's turned him down, and I get that. I'd rather be with Harlow as friends than ruin it and not be with Harlow at all. What they went through today seems really interesting, and she goes on even as we finish and I wash our plates.

"Wow. He really gets a lot of information in that course."

"Yeah, and you know what? There's nothing we've heard of so far that I think we wouldn't be able to do."

"You're not that far into it, but I hope you're right." Learning of something that might prevent us from joining The Games next time round would crush Harlow. It's what she's wanted for so long, and I get why, which is why I'm in it with her. Even if I don't have the same need for justice, I'd follow her to the depths of hell to protect her. "Nico doesn't know what it's for, right?"

She bites her lip before she answers, tugging on it with her teeth. "No, but I don't like being a liar. Although, he hasn't specifically asked. I think he's just happy to be sharing his work."

"And you don't want to tell him?"

"I know people are going to think we're crazy when they find out. I'd rather he didn't think that, at least not yet. Plus, it's safer for everyone to keep it quiet." She's right. Ordinary people avoid the literal battle for power that is hosted every five years, but Harlow could never be described as ordinary. The normal reaction to the rounds of endurance, brains, and combat that attract the most powerful men in the city is to avoid them. But she's running headfirst into them, determined to change the future of this city. And she's worrying about some reserved university student thinking she's crazy?

"You could ask him out, you know? You're not exactly shy."

"I know," she says quietly. "I kind of accidentally did earlier."

"And?" I hope my quick response is taken for a friend eagerly wanting to know rather than the real reason.

"He shot me down," she says with a shrug. "Basically said he can't wait for the sessions to be over."

I frown at her in confusion. "Ouch."

"Yeah. Whatever. I'm gonna head to bed." She stands to hug me, and I envelop her in my arms, pressing a kiss to her hair.

"Night, Angel." She murmurs a "night" against me before padding to her room and shutting the door behind her. Harlow's crush on Nico has never got her down before, but I guess this is the first time he's shut her down completely. Minutes ago, I was worrying about how Harlow having a boyfriend would affect me. Now, the thought of her being unhappy because of not having one has me hoping Nico does make a move. What is his problem?

Chapter 4

Harlow

I'M ON THE EARLY shift this morning, which means an eye-watering 6 a.m. start and spending the first half of the day with Fleur. The commuting rush is over, and I'm wiping the counter down when she stands next to me, hands on her hips.

"What's up?" I ask with a frown.

"I was just about to ask you that. That's your fifth sigh in the last ten minutes. It sounds like you've got the weight of the world on your shoulders." I didn't even realize I was doing it.

"I'm fine," I try to reassure her.

"No one who ever says the words 'I'm fine' is actually fine." I shrug in response, because it's nothing important. So my crush doesn't reciprocate my feelings. Big deal, Harlow. Talk about first world problems. I can't say I'm sulking because a guy doesn't like me without sounding like the petulant brat

I'm being, but Fleur doesn't let up. "Are we talking it out or drinking it out?"

My eyes flick to hers at the mention of a drink. Even remembering trying to drag myself through yesterday after the last night out doesn't deter me. I will never learn. "Drinking it is," she says. "I'll have a nap between my split shift, and you nap after yours." I smile at her instructions, happy to have something to distract me from moping. "That's more like it!"

A customer comes to the counter and I have to finish the conversation to serve, but I've got more of a pep in my step for the rest of my shift. It picks up again, and Fleur and Celeste swap over before she's back in what seems like minutes, signaling the end of my own shift. Being busy is sometimes a blessing.

"We'll pick you up at nine," Fleur calls as I leave, and I throw a wave over my shoulder.

I have a nap, as instructed, although I can't sleep for nearly as long as I'd like. When I wake, I make some dinner, leave Sawyer some leftovers in the fridge, and get ready. I give myself a stern talking-to in the process. I cannot let other people's feelings of me dictate my mood. So I have tiny crushes on two guys who don't have crushes of any size on me. This is fine. I am more than the men who do or don't want me. I'm being ridiculous. And tonight, I'm getting laid.

Opting for a black blazer dress and some strappy heels that wrap around my calf, I pair them with nude makeup and a big blowout. There's a knock on my door as I fix some stray hairs in the mirror, and I grab my bag, answering the door ready to leave.

"Wow. You look amazing."

"Thanks, Sawyer. So do you," I reply. He really does, in a white shirt that fits in all the right places and some dark navy trousers. "I didn't realize you were going out."

"It's Kevin's birthday," he says, and that rings a bell somewhere in my head. I'm sure he's mentioned his colleague's night out before. "I didn't know you were either."

"We only decided earlier."

"We?"

"I'm going with Fleur and Lee." Lee is Fleur's boyfriend, and he's a total sweetheart. He's fairly quiet but is always up for being a chauffeur/bodyguard for Fleur on nights out without dampening our vibe. "Where are you going?" I ask.

"Probably the same place you are—the Regency."

"That's not your usual spot." He shrugs.

"Birthday boy's choice. Do you want to jump in our car? They're two minutes away."

"No, it's okay. Fleur and Lee are already on their way. I guess I'll see you there, then?" He cups the back of my head and lays a kiss on my hair as his phone beeps.

"See you there."

Now I remember why I don't go out with Sawyer. This is hell. Forget everything I've ever said about a bad time. My personal torture is being forced to watch a whole line of girls take their turn to hang off Sawyer and essentially peacock as he takes his pick for who he'll fuck tonight. This is not distracting me from my other guy woes, and unsurprisingly, my mood is sour, but I can't explain why to Fleur or Lee. No one knows quite how deep my feelings go for Sawyer, even if I joke with Fleur about perving on him. This won't do. I need to get laid and get Sawyer's possible conquests out of my brain.

"What about him? Two o'clock?" I take a sip of my drink and subtly look in the direction Fleur gestures. There's a guy with a receding hairline and a beer gut staring straight over here.

"God, Fleur, I'm not that desperate."

"Well, there are plenty of better specimens around us right now." I give her a withering glare, but she grins back at me. There's no way I'm hooking up with someone Sawyer works with. That's a straight-up no.

"What about the guy coming in, the one in the cheap suit?" I take a glance expecting to shoot down Lee's suggestion after that description, but I'm pleasantly surprised. The guy is probably about my age and has a strong jaw and dark hair he's combed back, albeit with way too much gel. He reminds me of a used car salesman and is probably cocky as hell, but that's what I need tonight. Someone who's confident in rocking my world, who I hopefully won't have to take home to get him to do it—I literally just changed my sheets. Well, Sawyer did. The guy is walking in and heading to one of the tables with a group of people already there.

"Not bad. You might be able to remain my wingmen after all. Drink, anyone?" I down the last of my cocktail and head up to the bar, settling myself just in front of the guy's table. He appears next to me as I order, and in the mirror behind the barman, I see him do a double take when he sees me.

"Can I get these?" he asks me as the barman steps away to make them, and I turn to him, plastering a wide smile on my face.

"Really? Thank you . . ."

"Steve." He holds out his hand to shake. "You're welcome . . ."

"Lo."

"Nice to meet you, Lo."

"Likewise."

He looks behind me and frowns as a hand comes around the side of my neck, fingers tracing as I swallow.

"You okay, Angel?" is murmured huskily into my ear, and dammit, that tiny move does more for me than anyone else in this bar. I can't even *see* him, and yet his touch and his voice have taken my breath away.

"Yeah." I turn and look up at him as if he's my sun, which probably isn't too far off. He looks down with the same reverence, and we lock eyes for a minute as my awareness of everyone else in the bar disappears. He leans in, and my eyes flutter half-shut as, for some insane reason, I think he's going to kiss me. And god, I really want him to. Every molecule in my body is straining toward him, but his lips don't meet mine. Instead, they softly land on the same spot he kissed me in our apartment.

"He's gone," he says in a louder voice, dropping the act. "Let me know if he bothers you again."

Disappointment crashes down on me like a physical force, but I somehow manage not to buckle, and annoyance filters in through my lusty haze. Haven't I just spent the last couple of hours watching every girl in here paw at him? Yet I needed saving from a guy buying me a drink? No thanks.

"Thanks," I start innocuously, turning back to the bar and downing my drink. "But I didn't need you to do that."

"You liked him?" he asks, his brows rising in surprise.

"I liked him enough." I shrug with a faux lightness I'm not feeling.

Sawyer's eyes change into something I've never seen before, and I can't figure it out after this many drinks without him spelling it out to me. He smiles tightly. "Okay. Have fun then, I guess."

I rejoin Fleur and Lee in the gym crowd, but when I see Steve go back up to the bar a bit later, I slide in next to him. It's stupid and childish, but now I have a point to prove, and more than an itch to scratch.

I lean close to make sure he hears me over the music. "I think it's my turn to repay the favor."

"Oh, no way," he says. "Girls who look like you shouldn't pay for drinks."

"I have to make it up to you somehow," I say coquettishly, laying a hand on his arm. I make myself sick sometimes—how easily I can act like this with guys I'm barely attracted to—but I know what guys like this one want, and it's the same as what I want right now. Might as well get there as obviously and quickly as possible. I'm not ashamed for being sexual and loving sex, I just wish I had someone I truly connected with.

Steve licks his lips and looks me up and down with a leer that I think is supposed to be sexy. We chat for a bit and I flirt like a pro, confirming I am in fact single despite what it looked like before, and laughing like he's the funniest thing in the world. My eyes ache from the strain of not rolling them. Eventually, I've had enough small talk. "I'm going to pop to the little girls' room," I say as I look up at him suggestively.

Of course, he's outside when I get out. I didn't doubt for a second that it would work. If only I could be this effective and confident with the right guys. But no, the goal of tonight is to *not* think about them, and to try to ease some of my horniness.

"Were you looking for me?" I ask.

He doesn't answer, instead pushing me back against the hallway wall and kissing me. Not the best technique, but he's forceful with his mouth against mine, taking what he wants. Hmm. Maybe we can work with this. I pull away and walk backward, pushing against the door I know leads to a supply cupboard. Don't ask me how I know, or why it's always unlocked. Steve follows me in and kisses me again. You'd hope his enthusiasm would make up for the lack of skill, but sadly not. There's a lot of tongue. I sit up on the low cabinet, and he's got himself out and hard within seconds, but I'm not mad at getting straight down to business. I'm not here for his company.

"Condom," I say determinedly.

"I don't carry them," he says with a shrug and a boyish grin, but this isn't my first rodeo.

"I do." Fumbling in my bag for one, I slide it onto him and wrap my legs around his waist as he pushes in. Not a bad size; better than Colin, anyway. But Steve's clearly all show and no tell, setting the most bizarre pace and rhythm. I lean back to try and improve the angle, but nothing. "Go rougher," I command.

"What do you mean?"

"Like, faster. Harder."

"Like this?" Considering nothing has changed, no.

"I need you to be rougher with me." He gets a bit faster and kisses me, and I worry he might finish already and leave me hanging. I can't deal with that tonight. Pulling back, I yell against his lips, "Steve, rougher!" He smashes his mouth back to mine before biting my bottom lip so hard it splits. I gasp at the sting of pain and push him away, licking at the tender spot and tasting copper. He freezes, seeming to realize that he may have gone the wrong route, and stares at me in horror. "I think we're done," I say as I push myself off the cabinet and stand.

"Shit. I'm so sorry, I panicked."

"It's okay. No hard feelings." I mean it, too. It's not his fault he was never going to live up to what I want. He's not *who* I want. "See you around."

I escape the cupboard before he's even put himself away and make my way back to Fleur and Lee.

"Fuck, what happened?" Fleur asks as I stand with them.

"Is it that obvious?" I prod at it with my tongue and wince. I didn't even check it before I came back out.

"Yes! Did someone hit you?"

"No, of course not. It's fine. You don't need to worry about me." I give what I hope is a reassuring smile, but it turns to a grimace when it pulls on my tender lip.

"But I do." She's frowning at me, and all of a sudden, this whole night seems decidedly un-fun.

"I'm gonna head out. Do you mind?"

"No, of course not. Sawyer left when you disappeared, by the way. He asked us to make sure we took you home. We'll leave now too."

"Are you sure? I don't want to cut your night short."

"It's fine, we're done anyway."

Half an hour later, I'm washed, changed, and cozy in bed. If only the screeching from Sawyer's bedroom would stop, I might almost relax. Speak of the devil—five minutes later my door swings open and he strolls in, freezing when he sees me.

"Oh, sorry, Angel. I didn't hear you come back."

"Not surprising," I say bitterly. Unfair, but it's out before I can help it.

"She's kind of loud, right?" He cringes as he sits down on the side of my bed, misinterpreting my hostility. I can just see his profile in the dim light. I have no idea what possesses me to continue, but my mouth is doing its own thing tonight.

"You don't like them loud?" I say.

"I like them authentic," he replies.

"Fair."

"I thought you might come back with someone." It's not a question, but I answer anyway.

"Nope." He turns to face me at my simple answer, frowning when he catches sight of my lip now that he's closer. He reaches out, pinching my chin between his thumb and finger, and turns my face so he can see the side in the low light.

"What the fuck happened to you?" Carefree Sawyer is gone instantly.

"Nothing important." I try to pull free, but his hold is steady, even if it softens.

"Someone hit you," he states angrily.

"No, they didn't."

"Harlow, what happened?" he demands. I know he won't let it go, and I also know I could lie to him, but that's just not us.

"Someone bit me." The furrow in his brow deepens, but before he can explode, I continue. "In fairness, I practically asked him to."

"Him? Was this some kind of sex thing?" He looks at me with disgust, and my hackles rise.

"Don't judge me."

"Was it that tool at the bar? What the fuck are you doing with these losers?"

"You're one to comment, hiding out in my room with your dick still wet while she leaves."

"At least she came," he replies. Shame blankets me, and I hate it. I want to crawl out of my own skin. How does he even know that? If he was fishing, then he hit the nail on the head.

"Well done you. Get out." He leans his elbows on his knees and rubs a hand down his face. "I mean it," I continue. "Fuck off, Sawyer. I'm too tired and frustrated because I didn't *come* for this shit."

He turns back to me, eyes blazing as he stares at me. For a second I think he might offer to help me out, but that's ridiculous. With a sigh, he stands up and leaves.

Even as tired as I am, I can't sleep. Half an hour later, after I've listened to his conquest leave and the shower go, he crawls in behind me. I'm still awake and am enveloped by the fresh scent of our shower gel.

"I'm an asshole," he whispers. "I'm sorry. I just hate to see you marked by some random person."

I don't answer, because I don't have anything to say to that. What is happening? We don't argue. Ever. It feels like there's a tiny wedge between us, and I have no idea how to stop it, even if I'm clinging to him with both hands. Am I second-guessing everything because my crush is growing out of control? Or does he feel it too? He settles in with his arms wrapped around my waist and drops a kiss on the back of my neck before we both fall asleep.

Chapter 5

Sawyer

I WAKE UP FROM a very not-safe-for-work dream about my favorite blond bombshell, and it's clear why when the ass writhing against my crotch continues in real life. *My god.* I have the willpower of a saint. Gritting my teeth against the grinding of her hips, I try to go against my inherent need to sink into her, and instead move away. I'm hoping to get out before she wakes so it's not awkward, but when she moans lightly, my progress is thwarted when I nearly combust. Pressing against her to ease the ache slightly, I have to clamp my lips between my teeth to hold in a groan. Suddenly, she stills, and I know she's awake. Closing my eyes, I give her the chance to leave instead, and she takes it, jumping out of bed and running out of the room. Okay. So not sinking into her was the right call.

I wonder what's got her so wound up, and then I remember last night and what a prick I was. I can't believe she's letting guys rough her up. It's not that I'm kink shaming her—at all—but if that's what she likes, then she deserves to be with someone trustworthy and decent with this shit. She doesn't need to settle for these pricks. She could get any guy that she wanted. I know her upbringing was bound to leave commitment issues, and I get that, but I don't see why she's settling for people that won't even get her off. I'd never actually had that confirmed until her reaction last night.

The shower turns on, and the image of Harlow getting off *now* under the stream of water comes straight into my mind. I need to get over this infatuation with her, or at least hide it better. She ran the second she realized I was here with her. Still, I want to stalk her into the shower and give her a hand. What I wouldn't give to make Harlow come, to watch her face as she orgasms and listen to the sounds she makes. *Fuck.* Now my hard-on is going nowhere.

I get up and head back to my room, setting up the coffee pot in the kitchen on the way. I brought fresh sheets in when I showered last night and so get to changing them now. I hate to keep the same sheets that someone else has been in. I like my bed to smell like our home—our smell—not some random woman. Getting dressed, I head back out and make us some breakfast. She's acting normal when she joins me, so I guess she believed I was still asleep.

Making things awkward between us by letting her know how I feel is my biggest fear. We have such a good thing going here that I'd never want to be the one to ruin it by being predatory. She needs someone she can depend on, and I'm proud to be that person, always. Although, her split lip does look sore, and the animal instincts inside me want to grab her and keep her safe in my bed for the foreseeable future. I don't mention it again, hoping she's forgiven me for being an asshole about it last night.

Harlow leaves for work, but I've only got a few classes this afternoon, so I plan to chill on the sofa before running some errands. Flicking on the TV, I cruise a few channels before the news catches my eye. It's not normally something I care about, but this is the local segment, and they're discussing the Guards. The report is on a brawl that happened overnight. As much as they try to make out that people kicked off against the Guards, which turned into an ugly public brawl with people ending up in the hospital, anyone who lives here would know that it was the Guards causing the damage. It's not said outright for fear of retaliation.

My attention is stolen when I hear banging outside. I intend to ignore it, but when it continues, I poke my head out the door to check it out. I see a girl across the hall unsuccessfully trying to push a sofa through the doorway, and just as I step out, a guy runs up the stairs.

"Didn't I tell you to leave it for us? I only had to take a quick call," he says.

"I can do it."

"Clearly, and the dented door frame agrees," he deadpans. He sees me standing there and acknowledges me with a nod and a rueful smile. "Hey, dude, sorry about the noise. Liv isn't the most coordinated of people."

Liv turns and grimaces at me, but before anyone can say anything else, another guy comes up the stairs with an armful of boxes and puts them down on the landing.

"You're so impatient. How have you disturbed our new neighbors already?" Now I can see him better, he looks crazily similar to the other guy, both a similar height to me with dark skin and short cropped black hair. They have to be twins. The newer guy is wearing a tank, and he has a heap of tattoos covering his arms. I want to take a closer look, but that's a weird first thing to ask when you meet someone, right?

"You haven't disturbed me. I wasn't expecting new neighbors until the weekend, that's all. I'm Sawyer."

I offer my hand, and the new guy shakes it. "Ezra. This is Liv, and Eli." The woman does a little wave, and the guy trying to step over the sofa to reach the other end salutes. "We all happened to score a last-minute day off so thought, why wait?"

"Do you need a hand?" I ask.

"Are you sure?"

"Yeah, of course."

"There's loads more in the truck, in that case. Liv can show you down while I get this in with Eli without damaging the whole apartment."

Liv rolls her eyes good-naturedly as she replies to the instructions. "Fine, I know when I'm not wanted. Are you ready?"

"Two secs." I put the door on the latch and throw some shoes on before following her down to the street, where there's a huge open moving truck.

"Just grab anything you can, thanks." By the time I've taken my first load up, the sofa is inside, so I put the boxes on the living room floor rather than on the landing. We all do a few more trips—Ezra, Eli, and I wrestling with the furniture between us—and as we drop the second sofa inside, Eli flops down into it.

"Time out. I need a drink."

"I bought supplies," Liv announces as she spins on the spot, "but I can't find them."

"Let me grab some." I'm out and in my own apartment before they can argue, and I grab a selection of drinks. When I head back in, the chaos seems to be more obvious, and I know for a fact that the truck isn't empty yet.

"How much more are you planning on fitting in here?" I joke.

"Eli likes his stuff," Ezra comments with a long-suffering look.

"It won't be so bad once it's in separate rooms," Liv defends him, and I wonder what the dynamics are.

"Are you all moving in?"

"No. Eli and I are on the lease, but Liv'll stay here a lot. They're together," he says, nodding toward them both. "What about you? Who's in your place?"

"Just me and Harlow. She's at work, but I'm sure she'll drop by to say hi soon." These guys seem way nicer than our old neighbors, and it'll be nice to have people our own age so close.

"So . . . together?" Liv asks curiously.

"Sorry, she's nosy," Eli says.

"Clumsy and nosy," she confirms, spinning to face Eli. "You're really selling me well, boyfriend dearest." I smile at their gentle ribbing.

"No, not together. Just friends." It kind of pains me to add the second bit, but it's true, after all.

"Yes, a single guy! You'll have to show me the best places to go," Ezra says.

"For sure," I promise. "I should go, though, I've got to get to work."

"No worries. Thanks for the help. Hopefully we'll be done by the time you're back. If not, we'll try to keep the noise down." I wave away their concerns and leave to a chorus of thanks and goodbyes. I have a good feeling about them, and I can't wait to update Harlow.

When I eventually see her that evening, she looks wrung out. I meet her outside the coffee shop to walk home with her, as usual, but especially important after seeing the news earlier.

"Hey," she says with a strained smile.

"Everything okay?"

"Yep, busy day. You?" she asks.

"Wasn't too bad. Our new neighbors moved in."

"Oh, yeah? Better than the old ones?"

"Lots better. I think you'll like them." I look down at her, but I can see she's only looking at the ground in front of her. She must be exhausted.

"That's exciting. I'll go and introduce myself tomorrow—I just want to crash tonight."

"Movie night?"

"Sounds perfect." I was going to talk to her about the news, but now I don't want to stress her out. It's not important right now. It can wait.

Chapter 6

Harlow

IT'S ANOTHER EARLY SHIFT for me today, and the first half is with Brian. He's lovely but very quiet, and I feel like the hours always go slower working with him or Celeste, no matter how busy we are. The rush comes later, with it being a weekend, and he must slip out at some point because he's suddenly replaced with Nico handing over the coffees. That's more like it. He frowns when I smile at him, pulling on my split lip, but it's too busy to get into it, thankfully. I can't wait for it to heal already.

We work like a well-oiled machine through the lunch rush, and I'm in the zone as I hand over a large toffee nut latte.

"Good afternoon, what can I get you?"

"Your number would be great." This isn't the first time I've heard that line, and it still surprises me that people would try it during a busy rush. Preparing my normal "that's not on the menu" shutdown, I make the mistake of looking up at the perpetrator before saying it and am temporarily stunned. Just temporarily, but enough for my slack jaw to be obvious, as his face breaks out in a godlike grin. You know the guys you see that are like, fuck. And then they smile and they're like, *fuuuuuuck.* Yep, that's this guy. He has deep skin, with full lips and piercing eyes that should look feminine but somehow don't. His short hair matches the neat stubble on his jaw, and his wide smile shows perfect teeth. Where the hell did this guy appear from?! Eventually, I pull myself together and manage a reply.

"I've never heard of that. Is it a latte?" His grin doesn't falter, and I feel myself flush at his attention.

"A latte would be great."

"Anything else?" He raises a brow at my offer, and I blush, imagining what else he could be thinking about wanting from me. His gaze flicks to my neck, where I know my blush is evident, and I clear my throat.

"Nope, not now I've been crushed after shooting my shot." He leans down on the counter, bringing him closer to my height. "Remind me not to use a cheesy pickup line again."

"I have a pen here, I could write it on your hand?" I offer primly.

"Your number?"

"The reminder." He stands back, clutching his chest as if wounded by my refusal.

"Ouch."

"You're a big boy, you'll get over it."

"That I am," he replies with another one of those magic grins, and I gently bite down on my bottom lip to stop from grinning wildly back at him. When Nico clears his throat behind me, I jump, the spell well and truly broken. I've never flirted with someone at work before, and especially not in front of Nico. I feel like I've been caught out being unprofessional and holding up the queue. I finish taking the guy's order, and he goes to wait at the end of the counter, but I can still feel his eyes on me. Unfortunately for my productivity, he chooses to sit in to enjoy his drink, and I get more and more flustered as the time goes on. Thankfully, the rush dies down.

Nico has to head out the back to get some more clean mugs, but Brian comes back through the door a minute later to relieve me for the second half of his split shift as I'm taking coffees over to a table. I'm smiling at him as I cross the floor just as a customer stands up and steps right into my path. The whole tray is pushed back into me, and the contents splash over my chest and hand. *Shit* that's hot.

"Watch where you're going, you stupid bitch!" The guy who may have just given me third-degree burns shouts in my face as he shakes a few lone drops off his jacket. I hear the screech of chairs against the floor, but I'm already rushing out the back, skin on fire, unhooking my apron from around my neck as I step through the door and strip my top off. Quickly running it under the cold tap, I press it against my chest before soaking it again and repeating, and I sigh at the little bit of relief.

"What the fuck?"

I spin with a gasp, water running down my front and into my waistband, to face Nico. I'd completely forgotten he was back here. I glance down at myself, but he can't see anything now I've got the wet top scrunched against my chest. "What happened?" he asks.

There's muffled shouting coming from the coffee shop, but he ignores it, coming toward me with concern in his eyes.

"Just a spillage. A hot one."

"Shit. How does it feel?"

"Not too bad. Good thing it wasn't extra hot, huh?" He doesn't laugh at my weak joke, his brow furrowed.

"Can I check it out?" I nod, because he's so close now I can smell him and "no" is no longer in my vocabulary. Not that anything is happening between us. He's Nico, my friend. Just friends. He's showing friendly concern over my possible injury. It's a lot easier to pretend to convince my head than my hormones, and my heart rate picks up at his closeness. Pulling my crumpled top away, I glance down as he does, taking in the red mark over my chest and the tops of my breasts. I hiss at the slight sting of the air on the fresh burns.

When I look back up, happy it doesn't look bad enough to blister, he's still inspecting it.

"Looks okay, right?"

His eyes snap back up to mine and he nods with a swallow, his voice rough. "Yeah. Yeah, it looks okay. I'd hold the compress on a bit longer. What happened to your lip?" Explaining what really happened is the last thing I want to do, but Brian comes through the door and I realize I'm standing a foot away from Nico, half-naked. Turning back to the sink to run my top under the cool water again, I wring it out and cover myself with it before turning back around.

"You should've seen how that guy just tore him a new one," Brian says.

"What guy? Who?" Nico asks.

"A customer completely ripped into the guy who shouted at her. I thought he might wet himself."

"Who shouted at you?" Nico asks me with a frown.

"No one, it doesn't matter. Has he gone?"

"The shouter has. There's a gorgeous guy who wants to check if you're okay. I'd take a burn or two to get his number," he mutters, almost to himself.

"Okay, thanks." I smirk at the idea that maybe Brian has a personality after all, even if it's only when there's a hot guy at stake. Is he talking about the guy from the queue? He must be, unless there's some modeling convention happening nearby that I'm unaware of. "I'll be a minute," I say. He leaves to cover the register, and I head over to my bag, pulling out my gym kit. There's a fresh T-shirt in here somewhere for after my workout.

"Do you want me to get rid of him?" Nico asks, but I shake my head.

"No, it's fine."

"Are you sure? Just cause he shouted at someone for you doesn't mean he can harass you." I turn in shock.

"Harass me? What do you mean?"

"I'm just saying, he's not *owed* anything." He says it in such a way that we both know what he's insinuating.

"Yes, thank you, Nico. I'm not about to rip my clothes off in gratitude." He raises a brow and pointedly looks at my half-dressed state, and my eyes narrow. "Is there a problem?" Since when did he get so judgy?

"Not from where I'm standing." My whole body flushes. That's the first time Nico has ever made a comment like that. His eyes are molten, but they soften slightly. "Look, I'm not trying to judge you. I'm trying to look out for you."

"Well maybe don't," I say. I know I'll regret it later, but oh well. He's caught me off guard.

"Harlow—"

"Can I get changed so I can go, please?" I ask, gesturing down at the top I'm still holding to my bare chest. He holds my eye for a second, and his jaw ticks as a ridiculous warmth rushes through me at the determined look in his eye. Assertive Nico has my pulse quickening.

"Yeah, sorry," he says, sounding anything but sorry as he leaves, and I sigh. I'm not trying to pick a fight with him. But really. Who does he think he is? I'm a grown adult, he's got no business telling me what to do and not do. What is it with these guys thinking they know best?

I take my stuff to the toilet and change into my gym wear completely, seeing as the water has dripped into my jeans too. Stuffing my work clothes into my bag, I head through the shop with a quick wave to Brian and Nico, who are dealing with the queue that formed during the drama, and meet the guy out the front of the shop.

"Hey," he says as he sees me, standing up from his casual lean against the wall. "How's the chest?" I raise my eyebrows, and he smirks. "You know what I mean."

"It's fine. I hear I have you to thank for defending my honor?"

"I'll take thanks in any way you want to give it." Normally I'd like that line and flirt right back, but now Nico's got into my head, and I don't say the retort on my tongue. Thankfully, his phone rings to save me from thinking of something else. "I've got to get this," he says regretfully as he checks the screen.

"No problem. I'll see you around?" He gives me a questioning look, but I'm already walking away toward the gym.

By the time I get to the gym, the adrenaline has worn off and my chest is really starting to sting. I'd usually work out in a sports crop, but I gingerly slip my T-shirt back on over the top when I realize there's no way to hide the red mark blooming across my skin. After the way Sawyer reacted over my lip, I don't want to get into what happened back at the coffee shop with him. It might've passed as a flush if I was already warming up, but right now? Never. If he thinks my added layer is unusual, he doesn't show it, seeming completely distracted. Maybe he wouldn't have noticed the mark after all. Just my luck, though, we're practicing close combat.

Getting up close and personal with a sweaty Sawyer could be used as self-discipline training. Feeling the hard planes of his body but not being able to *feel* the hard planes of his body has my fingers itching with the effort of not touching him. I'm slightly distracted by the cloud of lust filling my head when he bands me to him with a forearm just below my collarbone, and with the effort of keeping the hiss of pain in,

I push him away a touch rougher than I would normally. He looks concerned when I spin to face him.

"You okay?"

"Yeah, just some pent-up energy," I say casually, hoping like hell he believes me. He keeps eye contact for a second, but I can't. Lying to him is one thing, but looking straight at him while I do it? I can't. The next move has him coming down over me. He holds my shoulder against the ground firmly, the heel of his palm pressing into my injury, and I gasp. He wrenches his hand back like he's the one who's burned.

"Sorry," he says quickly, standing up and holding a hand out for me. "Did I hurt you?"

"No," I reply as I stand with his assistance. I don't know how to explain the reaction, but he jumps in before I can, clearly reading the situation wrong.

"I didn't mean to touch you like that." But it's hardly an intimate touch for us, why would he assume my reaction was to that? Is he seeing my crush? Can he tell I'm practically panting over him and is trying not to give me any mixed signals?

"Ready for some cardio?" he asks while I'm still questioning everything. That definitely wasn't in the plan—he never mixes sessions—and now I'm sure he's trying to make some space between us. Embarrassment floods through me, and my chest throbs from the sweat and the inadvertent pressure of my shirt and his touch. I just want to go home.

"Actually, do you mind if we call it early? I'm shattered." It's only ten or so minutes to lose anyway. His brow creases in concern and his mouth opens, but he stops himself from saying whatever he was about to say.

"Of course. I've only got fifteen minutes until my next class, so is it okay if you Uber home?" I assure him it is, not wanting to wait around for his next class to finish like I normally would. "I'll see you later."

Chapter 7

Nico

"Y̲O̲U̲'R̲E̲ S̲U̲C̲H̲ A̲ G̲R̲U̲M̲P̲. I haven't managed to drag you out in forever."

I smile over at my sister in the passenger seat.

"I'm not a grump. I'm really busy."

"I know, you're always either working or studying. I admire you, but you're so young. You need to have fun."

"Study—"

"Don't give me that crap about studying being fun for you." She rolls her eyes. "I know it's not *just* an excuse to get away from us, but it can't count as actual fun."

"I'm not trying to get away from *you*."

"I know, sorry. That was a cheap shot. And I don't blame you. I just miss you."

"I miss you too, but you know I'll be there in a second if you need me."

"I don't, not in that way. I may as well live in an ivory tower." I for one am glad of that, even if she's not. Being locked away is the safest place to be for the women in our family, but she doesn't need to hear that right now.

"You're out now, aren't you?" I remind her.

"Yeah, going for an old lady brunch with my brother," she scoffs. "It's not even bottomless."

"Weren't you just moaning about missing me?"

"You know what I mean." She shoots me an apologetic smile, but I do. "You know the only reason he keeps me locked away is because he's worried the Guards will get to me."

Okay, maybe we are having this conversation. I let out a heavy sigh at her bringing this up, but better to talk about it in the privacy of the car than once we're out of it. "I know, Clara, and it's shit. But—"

"No, Nico. What's shit is that he doesn't actually care about me getting hurt. We both know he treats women worse than what they'd do to me. He just can't bear the thought of the Guards having got one up on him. They'd see catching his daughter as a win, and that's all he cares about."

"He would care." She scoffs, and I don't blame her. I couldn't even bring myself to sound overly convincing. I sigh at the turn in mood, but the Closed sign on the coffee shop door pulls my attention away. I was trying to get a peek at Harlow through the glass as we went past. Pathetic, I know, but I'll take what I can get when it comes to that girl. But closed? It shouldn't be.

"Whatever," my sister replies sullenly.

"Sorry," I mutter distractedly as I park across the road. "Do you mind if I check in on the shop quickly?"

"God, even on your day off you can't turn it off, huh? You've got two minutes. I'm starving."

I agree with a nod and jump out, crossing the road to try the door. Yep, definitely locked. I know Harlow should be here, but I'm not sure who she should be with. No one called to ask me to cover, though, and I hope nothing bad happened. Using my key, I unlock the door and hear sniffling in the second before the bell rings, but it stops as soon as the sound rings out.

"Hello?" I call, my heart jackhammering at the thought of Harlow being hurt in here. She comes through the swinging door with her hand pressed to her chest.

"My god, you gave us a heart attack! I definitely locked the door."

I jingle the keys in front of me.

"Is everything okay? Who's us?" That's Fleur's cue, and she joins Harlow behind the counter.

"Sorry, it's my fault," she says.

"Are you alright?" I ask. She nods and wipes her eyes on her apron, clearly not alright.

"We'll reopen in a second, I just need a moment. We haven't been closed that long, and it was quiet, thankfully."

"It's fine. None of my business."

"Nico, you're a man," Harlow starts.

"Glad you noticed." I smirk at her and she averts her gaze, looking over at Fleur again. "Get a man's opinion," she urges her as Fleur sighs.

"Do you mind?" Fleur asks me.

"Nope, fire away."

"It's Lee. He's absolutely great. So lovely and attentive, can't do enough for me. But every so often he'll cancel super last-minute or get a phone call he absolutely has to take no matter what we're doing, but he never explains it. Then I feel overbearing trying to get answers, like I'm bugging him, but he never offers any reason and he'll go back to being great again like nothing happened. Does he not like me that much? Am I being paranoid?"

"He probably does genuinely like you," I offer as Harlow raises her brows in a *told you so* way, and Fleur relaxes with relief. "At least as much as he likes his other girlfriend." Oops.

Harlow's head whips round to glare at me.

"Nico!"

"Sorry, but you asked. Sounds like cheating to me." Her eyes narrow even further.

"There might be another explanation," she says.

"But it won't be any better. What could be a good explanation for that?" Neither of them gets a chance to think of one because the bell goes behind me, and Clara lays her hand on my arm.

"Hey, are you ready to go?"

"I'm going to get ready to reopen," Harlow says quietly to Fleur, and then she's gone. I want to chase after her and tell her it's not what it looks like—it's not a morning date after the night before or anything like that—that Clara's my sister. But what's the point of that? It doesn't change anything between me and Harlow. Maybe it's better that she thinks I'm taken, leaves less pressure on my ever-dwindling self-control.

"Yep." Fleur has turned to fiddle with the coffee machine, and I feel like I've been well and truly dismissed. "See you later, Fleur."

My sister blows out a breath as we pull away from the curb. "Wow. She was gorgeous. Remind me to knock three points off my self-esteem before the day is over." I know she's talking about Harlow. Not that Fleur is unattractive, but Harlow is something else.

"Oh, please. You're gorgeous too." She gives me a look like she doesn't believe me, but I don't push it. Harlow is another level, and Clara's my sister.

"At least tell me she's super shallow and annoying?"

"Not in the slightest," I say with a mix of awe and want in my voice, which of course my sister picks up on.

"Ew. Are you sleeping with her?"

"No!"

"But you like her?"

"Yes," I admit, but only because it's Clara asking. She huffs in her seat.

"This is like pulling teeth. What's the problem? Is this part of one of your great big thought-out plans?"

"It's not a plan, not this time. I'm not dragging her into my life."

"Barista Barbie can't hack the dark side?"

"She doesn't like that." I can see her questioning look in my peripheral vision. "*Barbie.* She doesn't like being called that."

"Of course she doesn't. If you like her, she must be pretty impressive."

"That she most definitely is."

"Not impressive enough to give a shot?" That's not the issue here at all. I've no question that Harlow could survive anything thrown at her. But why would I want to throw it?

"If you had any other choice, would you still want to be in this position?" I ask Clara. "To be part of our family?"

"Absolutely not. I get it. It just sucks."

"Yep."

My mood has dipped with the reminder of why I'm staying away from Harlow, but I try and hide it for the duration of breakfast. Clara doesn't get to leave the compound very often, and she doesn't need to spend her freedom watching her brother mope over a girl. We chat and laugh and eat huge portions of huevos rancheros, but I feel the strain of putting on this show every minute. As soon as I drop her off with her bodyguards to drive her back into the compound—no way I'm going there unnecessarily—I feel my whole body sag.

I drive back past the coffee shop, even though it lengthens my drive slightly, and park opposite to catch a glimpse of Harlow. The shop is back open, and there she is, behind the counter, smiling politely at her next customer. That's how she should be—living her normal life with her normal job and no danger, existing peacefully and radiating happiness as she does it. Even knowing that, I can't stop thinking about her. She's all I think about most of the time. The reason I study so hard is to make sure I know the answers when she asks me for help. She took an interest in my course, and I want to make sure I can give her any answer, fix anything for her, but I also want to risk it all and make my move.

I can't, though. I can't get her involved in this shit. I can't be the reason she's in danger because I couldn't keep it in my pants. But god, it's hard. She's the perfect juxtaposition, looking like pure innocence to the world with her bright blue eyes and blond hair, yet I know how intelligent and quick and funny she is—a side I don't think that many people get to see. And now I've seen another side to her, too: the flirty vixen. God, what I wouldn't give to be on the receiving end of Harlow's flirty remarks.

When I'm home alone in my own space, I let my mind wander to just how fucking good it would feel. Watching her look up at me through those fluttery lashes. The blush that *I* caused creeping over her chest. Biting her full bottom lip between her teeth. I've only ever seen her do that when she's worrying, but wondering if she does it when she's feeling coy too gives me a whole new fantasy. Predictably, my dick throbs.

Jumping into the shower, I imagine that I'll actually get to do this with her one day. Have her tan legs wrapped around me while I grab her tiny waist. *Barbie* is right, and it's not surprising it's the first impression people get about Harlow. She's so dainty, but if you paid an iota of attention to her as a person, you'd know she never gives off a vibe that she needs protecting. There's so much more going on behind those gorgeous eyes.

Now I picture those eyes staring up at me as she takes me into her mouth, plump lips swollen around me. That's enough torture for one day, and I spill into the steady stream of water, letting it drain before I wash myself. I have a physical *need* for Harlow that gets harder and harder to control. These sessions need to hurry up and be over so I have no reason to be alone with her.

Chapter 8

Harlow

By the time Celeste is taking over for the afternoon shift, Fleur is feeling better, no thanks to Nico. Of course, cheating is everyone's first thought, but when Fleur is already struggling to keep it together at work, it's not the best time to bring that up. I have to admit that I like his straight-talking approach, and maybe it wouldn't be so bad in a different time and place.

But I shouldn't be liking anything. His girlfriend should like it. I can't believe he has a girlfriend. And she's gorgeous. I bet she's clever too. A touch to the arm isn't exactly a sexual gesture, but it was so natural and comfortable, they have to know each other well. Leaving the shop, I'm too preoccupied by my thoughts, and I almost smack into someone walking past.

"Sorry," I blurt as I look up, and I jump when I realize who is in front of me. The guy from yesterday. "Oh, hi again," I add. His eyes don't hold any recognition, which is a slight hit to the ego. But, thinking about it, his eyes don't hold much emotion at all. Is he high?

"Hi," he replies, looking me up and down with the most obvious check-out ever. Gross.

"What are you doing here?" I ask.

"I'm meeting someone at the park." That's a bit further down the road, past the gym. "Why?" he says. "Do you want me to be here for you?" He doesn't ask it in a predatory way, but for some reason, he's not pulling off the charming flirt act today. Maybe it's because his eyes are so blank, missing the playfulness of before.

"Oh, you're here," Fleur says in relief as she opens the door behind me. "You left your keys. New friend?" she asks with a smile.

"No, he was just going."

His eyes narrow slightly, like he doesn't like being dismissed. "See you around."

Oh, god. Was Nico right? Does he expect something now, is that why the act has dropped? I'm sure he didn't even recognize me when I nearly ran into him. Thankfully, he carries on down the road.

"Is he a creep?" Fleur asks me quietly.

"I don't think so. He's the one who told the customer off about my burn."

"Well, he's definitely as hot as you said."

"Yeah, but I think I got the wrong end of the stick about him." Maybe I was having an off day before. Hearts and vaginas can be so fickle.

"Shame. Here you go." I smile at her in thanks as she hands me my keys, and I make my way home.

Sawyer messages to say he won't be home tonight, and I feel inexplicably lonely in our apartment by myself. I contemplate seeing if Fleur wants to go out, but I know she's probably not feeling it tonight, and really, neither am I. I'd only be trying to fill some empty space with lackluster dick. So, I stay in, cook some good food, and binge-watch a trashy series on Netflix. Great self-care *and* I don't need to change my sheets.

The next morning, I'm opening my apartment door when the guy from the café comes out of 2b, and I freeze. He really did seem harmless enough back at work the other day, but after yesterday, I'm slightly put off.

"Are you stalking me?" I demand, closing the door behind me so there's no access. I know I could probably defend myself against him, even with his large frame, but my adrenaline spikes at the thought of needing to.

"I could ask you the same question." He frowns.

"I live here."

"Harlow?"

"What the fuck?!"

"Sorry, I don't want to freak you out." He holds his hands up in a conciliatory gesture. "I live here." He points behind him with his thumb to the door he's just closed.

"Oh, really? Prove it. And I have pepper spray in my bag." No need to warn him I'm pretty good at self-defense just yet. Although it really would be a shame if I had to hurt him, he is *so* pretty. His lips twist as if he's trying to stop a smile, and I narrow my eyes at him.

"I'm glad to hear it. But I just came out of my apartment the same way you did. Prove you live there." I hold my key up, and his matches.

"Fine. And work was a coincidence too?" I say.

"Yep." He's looking really quite happy about the coincidence, and as our eye contact continues, I realize they're nicer today, warmer.

"I'm gonna go," I say. "I have work soon."

"Okay." He nods but doesn't say anything else, but as I put my keys away and start off down the stairs, he falls into step with me. When I turn toward the direction of the café, he continues walking with me, as if nothing is amiss. "What are you doing?" I ask.

"I'm walking you to work."

"Don't you normally ask people if they want to be walked to work?"

"Well, normally I would, but I thought you'd say no."

"So why are you?"

"Because I want you to give me a chance. For some reason, you seem pretty against that, so I'm starting slow."

"Why are you so desperate for a chance?"

"I don't think you're ready for that answer. Although, I would love to see that cute little blush again." As if he's summoned it, I feel my neck and chest heat, and his eyes zero in on the skin there, no doubt turning pink. The top I'm wearing isn't immodest by any stretch, but suddenly, I feel half-naked. His eyes move back up to mine and his face splits into a grin. Okay, so he's back to sexy charmer today. Noted. I turn my gaze back in front of us, and we walk quietly for the rest of the way as I drown in my thoughts.

So the gorgeous guy from the café is my new neighbor. Does that change anything? Maybe. But my mind is so mixed up about him. If I'd seen him at the bar, I would've made a move for sure, but I don't like to see people I meet at work because they know where I'll be most days. Now, surely the fact that he lives next door is another sign not to go there. And that's without adding in the weird interaction yesterday.

"I can hear your brain working from here," he says when we're nearing the coffee shop. I shrug.

"I've got a lot to think about."

"Such as?"

"Why I shouldn't share my inner thoughts with strangers." He doesn't get offended by this, throwing me one of his panty-melting grins that he really shouldn't be allowed to use so casually. They can be pretty devastating to one's self-discipline.

"We're not strangers, we're neighbors," he says.

"I dunno, you're pretty strange."

"Yeah?" He chuckles. "Never been described like that before." I find that hard to believe.

He opens and holds the door for me, and I pass him as quickly as possible, giving Fleur a pointed look when she spots us both. Her eyes widen, but I subtly shake my head so she doesn't worry.

Heading into the back of the café, I nearly bump straight into Nico. He holds me by the shoulders so I don't trample him, and my skin warms under his touch, not having expected him to touch me and being off-kilter from suddenly finding my new neighbor attractive again. I need to deal with these feelings—I'm getting more scattered and flustered by the day. My crushes are getting out of control.

"Sorry, in a world of my own," I mutter to him, not looking him in the eye.

"Are you okay?"

"Yeah, I'm good. You can get off if you want." I cringe when I realize what I've said and still can't meet his gaze. I'm a little bit early, and the bell dings on the counter to signal Fleur needs a hand, but I'm not ready yet.

"It's okay, I'll get that." He finally lets go of my shoulders, but I'm still not brave enough to look at him as he leaves. Using the silence to center myself, I take a few deep breaths. *Get a bloody grip, Harlow. Since when have guys had this pull over you? Are you fifteen?* The dishwasher starts beeping, so I make myself useful after putting my apron on and empty it, refilling it with what's on the side in here before taking a crate of clean mugs out. Nico takes it from me the second he notices, as usual, and I smile my thanks at him. The queue has appeared from nowhere, which is unusual for this time of day, and I join Nico by the coffee machine.

"You should run now, we've got this," I say. He looks guiltily at the door as more people come through it, but he's done his bit. "Go on, I know you have a class. We'll survive, I promise." He smiles as he looks down at me.

"Make sure you do. I'd be gutted to not get to see you again." With that comment, he swaps his apron for his coat out the back and shuffles out past the queue. I, of course, spend the next hour rerunning the scene through my mind, flipping from *definitely flirty* to *a friendly joke* and back again. I give three customers the wrong drink before Fleur makes me swap with her and just take the orders. When it finally calms down, we both know it's only a matter of time before people drop in for their commuting drinks, so we take the chance to grab ourselves something.

"Are we talking about tall-dark-and-handsome over in the corner, or no?" I choke a little on my drink when I realize she means my new neighbor, who is sitting inside with a tablet on the table in front of him and one of those digital pens. I assumed he'd grabbed his drink and gone when I was out the back with Nico, and honestly, I'm glad I didn't know he was here. I've been enough of a clusterfuck today as it is.

"He's my new neighbor," I tell her when I've ridded my lungs of coffee.

"Did we decide on creepy or not?"

"Not. Not today, at least."

"Result—booty call without leaving the building!"

"No, no booty call."

"What, why not? He hasn't stopped watching you all afternoon, and you were all coy when you came in with him earlier." I shrug, not feeling convincing enough to explain my too-close rule to Fleur, but she takes my nonanswer as one anyway. "Oh my god, you like him!"

"I barely know him," I scoff.

"That's why you won't give him a chance. You're always scared of the ones you actually like." Is that true? Yes, I'm crazy attracted to him, but surely I can't like him already. We've barely spoken. Also, he's got the whole Jekyll and Hyde act going. Maybe I need to face that head on?

"Don't psychoanalyze me," I joke with a gentle elbow to her ribs, and she grimaces.

"Sorry. But for the record, I say go for it." Just then, he brings his empty tray up to the counter. I catch Fleur's eye, and she winks as she goes out the back.

"Thanks," I say as I take it from him.

"Can I walk you home later?"

"I actually have plans," I say, and I find myself disappointed that I do.

"Oh, okay. Well, I'll see you around, Harlow."

"Look forward to it . . ."

"Ezra," he answers before blinding me with another grin. Then he's leaving, and Fleur is back with me a second later, joining me in watching him go.

"You sure can pick 'em, girl."

"What's that mean?"

"It means you seem to be a magnet for sexy-as-fuck men."

"Shame none of them are available to me. Speaking of, are we still on for dinner? I've been looking forward to Thai food all week."

"Of course. Thanks again for coming. Lee was stuck for who to set him up with."

"No worries. Even if it's rubbish, the free food will make up for it."

Chapter 9

Harlow

THE BLIND DATE THAT I'd agreed to weeks ago is, in fact, rubbish. The only good parts of the evening were getting ready at Fleur's and the delicious food. Thankfully, it was a double date with Fleur and Lee, so we didn't just sit there in silence. I like my men with a little more substance and confidence. This guy resembled a wet lettuce. As I let myself into our apartment, it's quiet, and I jump when I see Ezra on the sofa, a game paused on the TV. He turns to smile at me as I walk in.

"Is breaking and entering not going a bit far?" I say.

"Is that not romantic these days?" he asks, humor in his voice.

"Not quite. I'm assuming there's a reason you're sitting in my apartment?"

"Yeah. Despite what you're clearly inclined to think, I'm not stalking you. Sawyer's gone across the road to grab some food."

"Oh." Sawyer had mentioned that the new neighbors were cool, but I didn't know they hung out. Although, we hadn't talked much in the last couple days. Sawyer comes in behind me with food from Chung's.

"Hey, Angel. You look incredible."

"I was just about to say that," Ezra complains.

"I'll take it from both of you." Yep, those are actual words that just came out of my mouth. They both snigger as I roll my eyes at my mistake, and I make my way toward my room but am stopped before I reach it.

"Chill with us. We're gonna put a film on." There's no reason for me to say no to Sawyer, and I really don't want to anyway. I've missed him recently, and he seems in a good mood.

"Okay, let me get changed." This dress may have received a welcome response from the guys, but it's not exactly lounging-on-the-couch material. After washing my face, I come back out in sweats and a tank. I settle next to Sawyer on the sofa, and he offers me his plate, but I honestly couldn't eat any more, even if it is Chung's.

"Did you eat?" he checks, always looking out for me.

"Yeah. We went for Thai."

"You and Fleur?"

"And Lee and his friend, a double date I'd agreed to a while ago." I say it offhandedly because there will most definitely not be a repeat. I already don't remember the guy's name, that's how awful I am. Ezra looks up and pins me with a glare that may or may not heat me.

"I hope you look that good when you're dressing up for me," he drawls, and I cock an eyebrow at him. "My housewarming party, of course," he adds with a smirk.

"Oh, I forgot to mention it," Sawyer says. "It's tomorrow."

"I'll try and make myself look presentable," I say impassively.

"Oh, please. Even in sweats, you look like a Barbie doll." Ezra says it with a hint of reverence, and for some reason, I don't hate the comparison this time.

"She hates that," Sawyer tells Ezra.

"Barbie? Why?"

"It's an insult," I explain, even though it didn't sound like it coming from his mouth. "Who wants to be described as an airhead? I'm so much more than my looks. Try complimenting my personality, my drive, my brain."

"They have Barbie doctors now. And racecar drivers. And chefs." He seems willing to carry on listing the offered professions as if it's proving something, so I jump in to stop him.

"You sure know a lot about dolls, but that's not what people mean when they say it."

"No. They mean you look like the perfect doll. No offense intended," he continues, "you really do. I think you're looking at it the wrong way. It can be an observation and not a criticism. I for one would be more than proud to have you by my side, looking like a Barbie or not. Might as well own it, you can't exactly change how you look."

"I could dye my hair, or cut it all off," I quip, but I'm feeling a stirring at his insistence to look at the positives in what he's said, even if he's so casually skipping over it. The fact that he wants me to see the good in it so sincerely makes me feel a type of way. Maybe I could be convinced to give it a chance.

"No," Sawyer interjects.

"I think Sawyer's a fan of the blond," Ezra says with a smirk. I grin over at Sawyer, but he's focused on his plate as if it's the most interesting thing he's ever seen.

"Well, now we've taken a deep dive into *my* head," I say, focusing back on Ezra, "what's *your* thing?"

"Go on a date with me and you'll find out."

"I don't date." That's not untrue in the slightest. I don't—and haven't—dated. Ezra looks to Sawyer for assistance, but he shrugs.

"I don't know what you want me to say. She doesn't. Tonight was unusual."

"You two have never hooked up?" Ezra asks lightly, but the atmosphere tightens, and Sawyer's face wears a horrified expression. His reaction snaps me out of the light, flirty mood like a stab to the chest. Not wanting to hear his rebuttal, I get in there first to clarify things for Ezra.

"No. He's like my brother. Are we watching this film or not?"

"Sure," Ezra agrees easily, "but this isn't over."

I don't focus an iota on the film, my chest swinging between swooning over Ezra's light banter and throbbing at the reaction from Sawyer to the idea of us hooking up. I really need to get over this thing with him. He's shown me more than once that we're platonic—nothing more—and I know it's my own crush putting interpretations of our interactions in my head and making me question his motives. I need to listen to Sawyer and respect his boundaries.

I brush my teeth once the film finishes and come out to Sawyer doing the dishes at the sink, Ezra taking my place in the bathroom.

"You heading to bed?" Sawyer asks over his shoulder.

"Yeah. I'm working early tomorrow."

"We'll keep it down. Are you gonna come to the housewarming?"

"Yeah, of course," I say.

"To see Ezra?" he asks. I frown at the question, but as he hasn't turned to face me. "You'll have to give someone a chance soon enough, you know. I know it scares you, but I think he's a good one." I instantly want to fight back against

Sawyer matching me off to someone and have to work to rein it in.

"You know him that well?"

"We've hung out a few times, but it's just a feeling I get from him, and from you when he's around." I think back to the flirty chat earlier and feel embarrassed for the first time to have been doing it in front of Sawyer. Sadness also creeps in at him trying to convince me to be with someone else, and I'm glad he can't read the emotion on my face.

"I'll think about it," I say. The water runs in the bathroom, and I take that as my cue to leave before Ezra rejoins us, feeling a little too vulnerable to be here with them both.

"Night, Angel," Sawyer calls as he carries on without hugging me goodnight, and that might be the biggest heartbreak of all.

I stew all morning about what I'm feeling. I don't know what was going on with Ezra the other night, but if I imagine that random meeting didn't happen, I can't deny I'm interested in him. It's made me realize that I can tell pretty quickly whether I have a connection with someone, and it doesn't happen very often. Even less often I have a connection with someone available and into me too. Part of me thinks

I should give Ezra a chance. I don't know why I'm so in my head about this. Our chemistry is insane, and I'm ridiculously attracted to him. Sex doesn't have to mean anything massive. He's put his cards on the table, so it's not like he's going to reject me. Why am I so nervous? Maybe I shouldn't give him a shot, though. What if I do, and suddenly I'm not attracted to him again?

As I'm coming up the stairs, a girl is waving and going down them. As I see his head over the top, crazy jealousy swirls up inside me. He's with someone else, but instead of being put off, I want to claim him, have him as mine. It can't be anything more than a booty call—he was at ours until late last night. Even though my stomach sours at the thought of him with someone else, he's not done anything wrong.

Without even thinking, I walk straight over and kiss him. He stands stock-still, not reacting at all, and the nerves come in again. Was he just playing? I'm not getting the same feelings I was from him looking at me now that we're actually kissing, and as he finally kisses me back, my heart plummets at the distinct lack of chemistry. *Shit!* This was a mistake. What is wrong with me?!

I pull back slowly and keep my eyes closed, praying for the ground to swallow me up. This is why you don't hook up with someone you're stuck around on a daily basis. I'm mortified. I finally look at him, and my stomach joins my heart in sinking when I see his eyes. They've lost their spark again. He's definitely on drugs, right? He has to be.

"What is going on?" I ask him.

"I was just about to ask that." I whip around to face the woman who had just left. Is she back to claim him? That was a bitchy thing for me to do, right? Well, she can have him now. Maybe I'll let her slap me to really cement the fact. "Is there a reason you're kissing my boyfriend?"

"Boyfriend?!" What a dirtbag.

"Eli, what is going on?" she asks *Ezra*.

"Eli?! You gave me a fake name?" Have I turned into a parrot? Is this all a big trick? She chokes a relieved laugh while my face flames.

"You're looking for Ezra, right? Eli is Ezra's twin." My mouth drops open. Ezra has a twin? Thank fuck for that. He's not on drugs—it's two different people. Of course it is. I'm so relieved I could collapse.

"And I'm Eli's girlfriend," she says, sounding much friendlier than I would in this situation. "Liv."

"Oh my god. I'm so sorry."

"Don't worry about it. They're mistaken a lot, though I have to say, this is a first." She mustn't have seen him kiss me back, or she'd be madder than this. I wonder how often they get confused and Eli goes along with it. "Harlow, I assume?" Even in the midst of my mortification, I warm at the fact he's mentioned me to them already. "So, you and Ezra?"

"Erm, no—not really. I'm not—maybe we just don't mention this again?" I hope, and they both laugh but don't actually agree. "I'm so sorry. Again. I'm just gonna go . . ." I gesture with my thumb behind me to my apartment, where I walk backward before slipping inside and headbutting the door as I close it. *Stupid, stupid, stupid.* What is wrong with me? I eat guys for breakfast. I don't get embarrassed or tongue-tied or anything else that's happened recently. I blame Ezra. And Sawyer. And Nico. *Eurgh.* I'm so screwed. I wonder if the nunnery would take me with my past encounters? Surely celibacy is my only way out of this.

I only get an hour out of the hope that Eli and Liv would keep it between us.

There's a knock at the door, and when I answer, Ezra is there with the biggest grin on his face. I groan and try to shut it again, but he holds it open and chuckles, so I go back to the sofa, throwing myself down dramatically and covering my face with my hands. I want to die all over again, the embarrassment coming straight back to the surface. The sofa dips next to me, and then Ezra's warm hands are around my wrists, bringing mine away from my face.

"You're so smug I could hit you," I tell him.

"I'm not smug, I'm happy," he corrects, but the grin doesn't go anywhere, and he even looks a bit flushed himself.

"It looks a lot like smug to me," I say.

"Well, maybe a little."

I huff and go to shove him, but he grabs my wrists again and pins them above me against the sofa cushions before leaning over and kissing me. I should've known the second I put my lips on Eli and felt nothing that there's no way he could've been Ezra. *This kiss.* This kiss is something else. What those smoldering looks had been promising. I feel it from where he's gripping me at my wrists all the way down to my curling toes as his mouth moves against mine with the perfect amount of force behind his soft lips. His tongue tangles with mine, and when he breaks away we're both out of breath. I'm sure my hooded eyes mirror his.

"I'm taking you on a date," he whispers against my lips.

"You really don't like asking, huh?"

"You have no idea." My stomach clenches at the unspoken meaning behind his words. "Tomorrow night."

It's kind of weird to think of an actual date and not just picking someone up at a bar for casual sex. Would it end the same way?

"I'm going now, because I'm trying to be a gentleman, but the way you're looking at me makes me not want to wait." I bite my lip against a moan, and he zeros in on it before letting one wrist go to drag my lip out gently. He leans in and slowly licks the small cut still lingering there with the tip of his tongue, and I clench *everywhere.* This time I do moan, and he stands up instantly, rearranging himself. "Nope. I'm going. I'll see you tonight for the housewarming party. Try not to kiss any more of my relatives between now and then."

I throw a sofa cushion at his retreating back, but I'm laughing when he leaves.

Chapter 10

Ezra

ELI IS FRANTICALLY CLEANING every surface possible before the housewarming guests arrive and snapping at us when we try to help, so Liv and I crack open a beer early and settle on the sofa.

"Who've you invited tonight?" she asks as we relax.

"Just some guys from the shop and next door."

"Harlow?"

"Yeah, Harlow," I confirm, not really wanting to dive too deep into this conversation.

"How does it feel knowing I kissed her first?" Eli smirks as he leans over the back of the sofa between us. Liv's reflexes are lightning-quick, and she smacks him on the shoulder before he can retreat.

"How does *that* feel?" she says.

"Don't tease her," I warn them both. "She's mortified."

"I think Harlow's a tough cookie," Eli reasons. I agree, but I don't want her to feel uncomfortable in any way here.

"I like her," Liv declares.

"The only time you met her, she kissed your boyfriend." Doesn't seem like the best start to me.

"Yeah, that was classic. But she was mortified, like you say, and you like her, so she must be pretty great."

"Some stunning family loyalty there." I grin over at Liv.

"Right, I'm done," Eli announces. "Don't touch anything while I change."

"Wear the blue shirt," Liv calls after him. "So . . ."

"So?" I ask, ignoring her questioning gaze for a swig of my beer instead.

"Do you like her?"

"Yeah, I guess. I only just met her, though. What's the big deal?"

"The big deal is you don't make an effort for anyone."

"Rude."

"Okay—you'd do anything for your family or friends," she acquiesces, "but I've never seen you try with a girl. You practically stalked Harlow for a date."

I shrug at her summary. Stalking's a bit of an exaggeration, but when you walk into your nearest coffee shop and see Harlow at the counter, you don't mind a bit of persistence to get a chance. And maybe her not falling at my feet adds to the appeal. Not that she needs any help, with her big, bright blue eyes that don't even look real, that bouncy ponytail I can't help but imagine wrapped around my fist, and those rosy lips that are sinful. Even imagining her now makes me want to fidget.

"She's cool."

"*Eurgh*, you're useless," Liv whines as she throws her head back against the sofa, and I chuckle at her sulking. I know she only wants to know I'm happy.

"I dunno. I don't want to jinx anything. It feels like it's something we should work out before I start blabbing."

"Okay, I can respect that."

"Can you?" I ask with an arch of my brow.

"*Yes*. Do you want another one?" She shakes her empty bottle at me, and I nod as I finish the dregs of mine. I get up with her and turn the lights and music on, setting the atmosphere.

"I can't believe you've set this all up already." Liv gestures around to the technology that fills our apartment, not just the stuff we're using for the party.

"I only had to reregister it to our new place. The setup is complete from before."

"Alright, brainiac, I don't need or understand the details."

Eli joins us as the door goes and the first of our guests arrive, which kicks off a steady stream of people arriving. I get lost in greeting friends and getting drinks as I introduce people. I'm mid-conversation with the guys I work with when I look up and see Harlow from across the room. I swear everything else fades out, the music dims, and I only see her.

She looks incredible, of course, in a deep green matching crop top and wide-leg pants, but I think she could be dressed in a bin bag and I'd still have the same reaction. She's laughing with Sawyer and Liv, and it's the most welcoming sight I've seen in a while. An elbow lightly connects with my ribs, and I look to the side to see Tom with a shit-eating grin on his face.

"Sorry, what was that?"

"Nothin'. Forget us boring buggers and go get your girl." He's heard all about her the last couple of days and doesn't need to tell me twice. Saluting him, I cross the room and make my way over as Liv leaves them. Harlow sees me before I get there, and that perfect smile widens, melting me. I take her straight into my arms, wrapping her up in my hold. It might be a bit presumptuous, but I want it clear to everyone here that she's off limits to them.

"When did you get here?" I ask as I pull back far enough for her to look up at me.

"Just a bit ago."

"Hey, man," I say to Sawyer with a smile.

"You good?"

"Not bad." I let Harlow go but keep my hand on her waist, right where that strip of skin is exposed. "Can I get you a drink?"

"I'll get it. Angel?"

"I'll come with you," she offers.

"I've got it. Wine?" Sawyer asks.

"Yes, please."

"Ezra?"

"I'm good, thanks."

When Sawyer walks away, I spin and lean my forearm against the wall, caging her in. Her big blue eyes look up at me.

"Was it something I said?" I joke, having cleared the group out in seconds.

"It definitely wasn't me. I'm a delight." I grin at her faux-haughty tone as I bring one hand down to cup her jaw, the other tangling my fingers in her hair.

"That you are." I finally lean in, kissing her like I haven't in weeks rather than hours. Her taste explodes on my mouth, and she slips her fingers just under my top to stroke my skin, causing little shocks wherever she touches. This is so natural and so right, I really wish we weren't with so many people right now.

"Harlow?" We're interrupted by a familiar voice, and I groan, tearing my lips away and leaning my forehead against hers. "I thought that was you." Straightening up, I turn to glare at my twin brother.

"Could your timing be any worse?" He blinks as if he can't understand what I'm saying, and Harlow takes pity, although her grip on my side tightens. I guess she's still working through some embarrassment, even if we all find it hilarious.

"Hi. Nice to see you again."

"Can I get you a drink?"

"Actually, Sawyer—" Her refusal cuts off as she notices Sawyer next to the bar the same time as we do, one of Liv's friends wrapped around him, his arm around her shoulder and their faces only inches apart. Looking back to her, I just catch the look on her face before she schools her features. "Oh. I guess he got caught up."

"We'll get it," I tell him. "I want to introduce Harlow to the guys anyway. Catch you in a bit." He opens his mouth to say something else, but I'm already pulling Harlow away from him by her hand.

"Which guys?"

"From the shop."

"What shop?" she whispers as we join the group. They look like the meanest bastards, with just as many tattoos as me, if not more, but are some of the nicest people I've ever met. I wouldn't have hired them if they weren't.

"My tattoo shop," I whisper back. "Hey guys, this is Harlow."

"Hi," Harlow greets them confidently, even as she squeezes my hand. She shifts slightly when they all gape at her, nobody speaking. Even Tom, who saw her earlier, is frozen when she's this close. The staring continues until I pointedly clear my throat, and then they all jump over each other to say hi and shake her hand. Fucking hell. At least I'm not the only one who's a complete sucker for her, although I hope I pull it off slightly better than that. Harlow chats easily with them, and she has them all laughing and eating out of her hand in no time.

Liv steals her to introduce her to a friend at some point, and I don't see her again until later, when I'm sitting on the sofa with Sawyer—who has managed to untangle himself from Liv's friend for a minute—and Eli. The girls wander over to us, eyeing the space between us one of them could probably fit into, but I pull her into my lap instead.

"What are you talking about?" she asks as she settles into me. The party has died down a lot by now, and there aren't too many people milling around.

"Just putting the world to rights."

"I don't doubt it."

"It'll be girls," Liv declares when she sits down next to Eli. "With guys, it's always girls. Which lucky one they're in love with today."

The same girl from earlier comes over and plonks herself in Sawyer's lap as both Sawyer and Harlow stiffen.

"Just one?" I joke, and the girl in Sawyer's lap scoffs.

"That's such a man thing to say."

"Why? I don't think you can only love one person," I continue, slowly stroking Harlow's thigh.

"Widows find love, even if they were married to their soulmate," Liv adds.

"I mean at a time."

"Like an excuse to cheat?" Liv asks, sitting up straighter.

"How do you not know this about him by now?" Eli asks her, and he's right. I'm pretty open with my feelings, but I guess we've never discussed it before.

"No. Not cheating. You have two parents, right? Which one do you love more?"

"Neither," Liv answers with a frown.

"Exactly. We have friends we love and family we love. Why do we have to only have one romantic love?"

Liv shrugs. "I don't think I'd be happy with only half of someone's heart."

"It's not a cake; it doesn't need to be split. What if it's infinite, it expands like the universe?"

"You're such a player," the girl on Sawyer's lap says with a glare, clearly cynical. "Is this a line to sleep with whoever you want?"

"I said love, not just hook up with." She's not happy with that, though.

"Men are pigs. What do you think?" she asks Harlow, who's been quiet so far.

"I can see both sides," she says thoughtfully. "I need time to think on it." I wonder what she really thinks.

"Whatever. Shall we get a drink, Sawyer?" the girl asks as she stands, hand outstretched to him, but he doesn't take it.

"I'm good, thanks." Her mouth purses before she drops her hand and walks away, and the group seems to relax without her here.

It's a few more hours before Harlow and Sawyer go back to their own apartment, and I keep Harlow on my lap the whole time. We don't get any time alone, but that's okay. I have big plans for us tomorrow.

Chapter 11

Sawyer

I've just made it back to my room after my shower when I hear the front door close, meaning Harlow is back from work. I was hoping to be out by the time she got back but procrastinated on my phone for too long and she's early, so now I'll have to wait for her to leave. Cowardly, I know, but something about her and Ezra seems to be more than her normal hookups. It's an actual date, not just someone she picked up at the bar. Harlow has never dated before, or even seen someone more than once. I can't stand to see her leave all dressed up for someone else, even if I did convince her to give him a shot. Seeing her so comfortable in his arms yesterday was tough enough.

We've also had an odd atmosphere between us recently—not helped by me practically feeling her up at the gym—even when I was actively not focusing on her. I can't keep her here, single, when she has a real shot at happiness, just because I have some unrequited feelings. Hopefully later she'll go back to his place, but I've got a booty call lined up either way to take my mind off her.

I guess it was always inevitable that she'd find someone. I can't believe no one has snapped her up sooner, but that doesn't mean I have to like it. I've tried to be her big-brother figure her whole life so that she has someone to rely on, and I'm not flushing that down the toilet because she's turned out really fucking sexy. Even as I tell myself that for the millionth time, I know it's so much more than that. I love every single thing about my angel.

I put a film on to kill some time, and once that is finished, it seems quiet in the flat, so I must've missed her leave. She normally says bye, but to be fair, I didn't even tell her I was here. I get dressed in some gray trousers and a black button-up shirt, adding a watch and some gel to my hair before grabbing my phone and leaving my room. Harlow pops her head up like a meerkat from the sofa, surprising me on my way to the door.

"Hey, what are you doing here?" I ask.

"I live here," she deadpans.

"Ha ha. I thought you had your big date?"

"It's not a *big date*, but also, I started my period." Damn.

"That's shit. How are you feeling?"

"Like crap, hence being on the couch." I should have known.

"How about I grab a duvet and we can order pasta and doughnuts?" I probably shouldn't offer, but it's such an *us* thing to do, I can't help it. Her eyes light up before they skim me up and down.

"Aren't you meeting someone?"

"No, not tonight."

"Really? You look hot."

"Well, thanks." I smirk, and she rolls her eyes with a smile.

"You know what I mean—you're all dressed up."

"That doesn't mean it's important."

I don't wait for her to say anything else, like trying to convince me to still go out, instead heading back into my room and changing into some sweatshorts. Harlow always runs cold for some reason during her time of the month, so she loves being under the duvet, but she's like a little hot water bottle.

I order our favorite takeout pasta and place an order for fried doughnuts to come half an hour later. We've been best friends since before she even started getting her period, when there was no one to look after her, so I happily stepped up. Now that we've also lived together for years, I've got this down. I throw the duvet over her head and go to the kitchen area while she arranges it and turns the TV on. She's picked a series by the time I come back with her actual hot water bottle, and she smiles up at me as I hand it to her.

"You are seriously the best," she says.

"I know," I agree as I settle down next to her.

"You were supposed to be meeting someone, weren't you? Did I ruin your plans?"

"I was meeting someone, but I'd rather be here."

"Am I the biggest cockblock known to man?" she asks, pulling an apologetic face while I laugh at her. The only reason I see so many different girls is so I don't pounce on her, or knock out some random guy she brings home.

"Something like that."

"The women of this town must hate me for taking up so much of your time."

I shrug. I have no real interest in those women for anything other than sex. She's chewing on her lip, so I wait for her to think through what she wants to say. "Do you agree with what Ezra was saying last night? About loving more than one person?"

"Yeah, I think so."

"Really?" She looks up at me and pulls her feet up under her.

"Well, it makes sense how he explains it." I shrug casually, because it does. I'd never thought of it before, but now, yeah. I could see that working.

"Yeah," she agrees. "Not that you have to be looking for more than one partner, but an open mindset like that is only positive, I think."

"Exactly. And if anyone has an infinite heart, it's you." Her eyes flick to me with disbelief.

"Hardly. I think mine might be a malfunction."

"No way. It's perfect. Just like every other part of you." She looks at me with a curious, searching expression, and I don't know how to answer it. I want to tell her that I love every single part of her, that I will spend my life showing her how incredible she is, that I'd die for just a tiny space inside that huge heart. But I already have it, don't I? I'm in there, I know that. Just not the way I'd like. But I'd rather stay there as family than leave.

She must see the drop in mood on my face because she frowns slightly, and her mouth opens, but the door knocks before she can say something. I jump up to grab it, and her face lights up when she sees the logo on the bag from over the sofa. We start the series with our food and don't mention the conversation again. Her reaction is the same for the second course, and it's worth every second.

Once we've finished, I take the trash out and refill the hot water bottle. I offer Harlow painkillers—even though I know she'll refuse, which she does—and sit down next to her. She tries to flatten herself as much as possible, so I kick my legs up and pat the sofa cushion where she can lay out in front of me. Giving me an appreciative smile, she lays on her side, and I put the water bottle against the small of her back, where I know she gets pain along with her cramps.

Laying down behind her as she burrows back against me, it sandwiches it between us. The shorts were a good idea. I place my arm over her and rub circles into her stomach. This is our ritual, but she's especially tense today, so the pain must be bad.

"Relax, Angel," I murmur against her hair. "You've got to breathe." She takes in a deep breath, letting her muscles relax as she exhales. It's not long before she's asleep, and I switch the show over to something a bit grittier.

An hour or so later, there's a knock on the door, but I'm anchored between Harlow and the back of the couch. Seeing as she tends to be a heavier sleeper, I risk calling out, "Come in." We never get visitors, so I'm hoping I've assumed right and it's either Fleur or Ezra. Thankfully, he calls "hi" back and walks round the sofa a moment later.

"Hey, man," I say lightly.

"Hey. I wanted to check on Harlow."

"Check on her, or check she didn't stand you up?" I grin at him as he narrows his eyes. "She's fine, just passed out."

"Are they always like this?"

"Yeah, she gets them pretty bad. If she pushes through it, she can get dizzy and nauseous. Fainted a couple of times when she was younger."

"Shit, that sucks," he says as he sits on the edge of the armchair, watching her. "What helps?" When he looks back up, he sees my shocked expression. "What? I plan on being around for a few more yet."

"Just a few?" The thought of Harlow going to someone else for this breaks my heart a little, but I can't keep her forever. And if he's willing to know what helps, then so be it. He stares me down without answering.

"Heat helps, which is why I'm sweating my balls off. She likes to be cozy, hence the duvet, and the hot water bottle is for her lower back or stomach. All of the carbs—we normally have pasta and doughnuts. Lots of hydration, and gentle exercise when the cramps aren't too bad. Then sleep. Harlow sleeps like the dead." He's listening intently, and I wouldn't be surprised if he whipped out a notebook and started taking notes. The bitter edge of losing Harlow softens at his concentration, even if only slightly.

"Okay, I can do that. I feel like you have all the insider information."

I do. I could tell him that she's scared to make mistakes because she's afraid of rejection. I could tell him she loves crispy bacon, banana cake, and clean sheets. I could tell him she's the most loyal person I've ever met, and that her heart matches her stunning exterior. But I don't. I can't force the words past the lump in my throat.

Harlow spins to face me, draping a leg over mine and snuggling into my chest, which could burst right now.

Looking down to make sure she's still sleeping, I tuck some loose hair behind her ear.

"Why aren't you two together?" Ezra's abrupt question has my attention back on him.

"We're like brother and sister." My go-to response comes out easily, and it sounds convincing, even to my own ears. I'm determined to stop this awkward road we're going down, and Ezra asking this again reminds me of her quick rebuttal last time and the way she's started flinching when I touch her anywhere outside of a hug. "And stop asking that, you'll make her uncomfortable."

"I don't look at my sibling like that."

"Maybe not, but she looks at me like one, and that's what matters. She's dealt with enough. I'm going to be the constant she needs without trying to get into her pants. And if you hurt her, I'll fuck you up, just like a brother would." He nods as I finish.

"Fair enough. Didn't you have a date tonight?"

"I canceled. How did you know?"

"Your *sister* told me."

"What's that supposed to mean?" He grins at me instead of answering. "Whatever. If you're staying, grab me a beer. I'm dehydrating in this heat. She's like a furnace." He does just that and settles further into the armchair after coming back with a beer for me and for himself.

Ezra does seem decent enough, like I told Harlow, and I'm glad she's giving him a chance. We've become easy friends pretty quickly, but can I really spend time with them if they're together? I want what's best for Harlow, but I'm not a masochist. I'd see her less, obviously. She'd probably stay at his, and he'd walk her to work in the mornings. I'm aware I'm getting ahead of myself, but the possibility of Harlow slipping away from me makes me want to hold her even tighter.

Chapter 12

Harlow

I WAKE UP THE next morning in a warm cocoon and sleepily blink my eyes open. They widen when I see Ezra sleeping in the armchair, one arm under his head and a leg thrown over the arm. What is he doing here? There's a scattering of bottles on the coffee table, so it seems he was here a while. Sawyer stirs behind me, and his arm tightens around my waist.

"Are you awake?" I whisper, not wanting to wake either of them if he's not. A quiet noncommittal hum vibrates into my hair, and I smile. "You've been bonding."

"Something like that," he mumbles back in a gravelly sleep-coated voice. "What time is it?" I snake an arm out from the duvet and tap my phone screen so it lights up with the time. It also shows a few missed messages and calls, but I'm in no rush to check them.

"Eight thirty. I slept for ages."

"Duh. There's no waking you once you're out." I wonder if he'll ever realize it's only with him, the only person so far I've trusted enough to slip into a deep sleep with. Nights are rough on my own. "Have you got work today?"

"No, I swapped with Fleur. I'll do her shift tomorrow." Ezra wakes up then, slowly blinking his eyes open against the light and realizing I'm awake.

"Morning, Sleeping Beauty," he says with a slow-growing grin that feels like the sun coming out. I can't help but grin back at him. He fills me with a sappy glow. "How are you feeling?"

I was slightly worried he'd be irritated at having to wait for our date, because most men I've seen haven't appreciated waiting for sex, but he doesn't seem to be. It also makes me feel awkward that I make such a big deal about my period, but honestly, it knocks me for six every damn month. Plus, being abandoned by an addict parent can make you paranoid about taking medication, even if it's only painkillers.

"Better, thanks. What are you doing here?"

"I came to check on you last night, and then Sawyer begged me to stay and keep him company."

"As if," Sawyer drawls from behind me, neither of us having sat up yet, and Ezra fights a smirk at the reaction. I love that they became friends so fast, even before I met Ezra, and it's not awkward for my date to be sitting across from where Sawyer is essentially spooning me. That should be awkward, right? Not for much longer, though, because Sawyer drops a light kiss to the back of my neck and then rolls away, stretching with a big yawn. I can't help the way my eyes fall closed when his lips press against my skin, and when I open them, Ezra's gaze hits me.

"I need to get my shit together," Sawyer declares. "I've got work. Do you want to skip our session today?" Sawyer climbs over me and stands, and I work hard to keep the saliva inside my mouth. He is something else, and his gray sweatshorts show off his tanned, chiseled muscles to perfection. Thankfully, I think he's blocking me from Ezra's view, so Ezra doesn't catch me checking him out.

"I shouldn't. Gentle exercise is good for cramps, apparently," I whine. I've never found these benefits true, even when I do manage to convince myself to do it. Sawyer chuckles as he heads to the shower, and I stretch and sit up, meeting Ezra's gaze again. "Did you have a good night? Sorry about our date."

"Yeah, Sawyer's a cool guy. Don't be sorry, we'll do it soon. Don't think you're getting out of it."

"Wouldn't dream of it." I grin back at Ezra, who stands and stretches, showing enough of his impressive abs himself that I nearly drool for the second time in two minutes. When I pull my eyes back to his, he's smirking down at me. "Good. Thought I'd been outdone there for a second."

I frown in confusion, my brain not working so early, and he leans down to kiss me. Just a light peck on the lips saves me from morning breath embarrassment, and he's off toward the door. "I've got a half-day today. Want me to come keep you company later?"

"I'd like that," I call after him as he waves and leaves. I reach for my phone and catch up on my messages while Sawyer showers, and then jump in after him, even though I'm definitely planning to put on some fresh pajamas for the day. Maybe I've decided against the workout already . . .

I join Sawyer in the kitchen as he's pouring coffee, one in a thermos for him and one in a mug for me, which he hands over.

"You're the best. Thank you."

"Knew you wouldn't make a workout this morning. I'll see you later, okay? Relax. Get some rest."

I nod as I tentatively sip my drink, the scalding heat not putting me off the first taste. Sawyer grabs his bag and opens the door to Nico, hand poised to knock, and both guys jump.

"Shit, sorry," Nico says, and I'm surprised to see him.

"No worries, man, I'm just heading out." Sawyer steps past him and leaves, and I join Nico at the door.

"Hey," I say curiously. I'm not sure he's even been here before, other than to drop me off out the front.

"Hey. How are you feeling?"

"Not bad, thanks. Sorry for bailing yesterday."

"It's fine, you didn't even have much longer left." That was true, but I hate leaving someone to close up alone. "I wanted to drop this round for you." He holds out a takeaway cup and a box, which I stare at dumbly for way too long. "It's your usual." He says that like it's not a big deal, but I'm pretty sure that means a caramel latte and a slice of banana cake from the café, and if there could be love hearts in my eyes right now, there would be. I finally take them from him.

"Wow! Thank you. You really didn't need to do that. Did you want to come in?"

"No, it's okay. I've got class in between the split, but I'll see you." With that and a smile, he's off, leaving me blinking after him for a moment. That was odd. But in a good way. I take my goodies back inside and put them next to the mug of coffee Sawyer made me. Physical representations of how two of the guys I have unreciprocated feelings for still care for me. It might not be how I would prefer to have them in my life, but this is pretty damn nice anyway.

I spend the morning doing absolutely nothing, which is unusual for me. I'm nearly always on the go, or getting some training or studying done, but today I just be, and it's definitely needed.

Ezra joins me again in the afternoon and brings a late lunch with him. Are these guys trying to fatten me up? Crossing my legs underneath me, I sit down on the sofa with my huge sandwich and second slice of cake of the day, and he sits back in the armchair. Looking up from my plate, I catch him watching me.

"What?" I ask, smoothing my hair subconsciously.

"Nothing," he chuckles. "You're really fucking cute."

"Cute?" Bare-faced and in cozy pajamas, it may well be true, but it's not the first thing you'd like the guy you're crushing on to say when describing you.

"Yeah. How are you feeling?"

"Okay, thanks," I say. "It's not a big deal." I shrug lightly, not wanting to seem like I'm overexaggerating.

"It sounds like it is. I've been learning the tricks of the trade from Sawyer."

"What does that mean?" I ask suspiciously.

"He was telling me how to help."

"Which is why you brought carbs and dessert?" I check, eyebrows high.

"Yeah. Is that okay?"

"It's okay." I manage to get the words out through my huge grin, wishing like hell I could thank him in a way that included less clothes. The air seems charged, all of a sudden. How do I feel so hot clutching a plate full of cake and bread?

"Stop looking at me like that," he warns me.

"Like what?"

"Those eyes are going to get you in trouble."

"Me or you?" I check, not taking them off him. He blows out a breath, and my phone ringing makes me jump. I reluctantly break eye contact and see that it's Sawyer.

"Hey," I say to him.

"Hi. I'm just about to go in for my last workout. Sure I can't tempt you for some training after?"

"Do you want to go to the gym?" I ask Ezra, holding my hand over the speaker.

"Sure," he answers back. "After you've eaten."

"Okay, fine," I say back to Sawyer. "But only because you all keep feeding me."

Chapter 13

Harlow

THE NEXT DAY, I'M back to work bright and early. I'm stupidly buzzed, but I'm trying not to acknowledge the fact it's because of my date with Ezra we rescheduled for later today. The gym session with him and Sawyer ended up being so fun, probably because I only worked out very lightly and we all chatted more than we exercised. Ezra fits in with us so easily, you'd never know we've known him for such a short amount of time. It feels like forever.

One of my bad traits is not liking to get too excited about things—because ninety percent of the time you get let down anyway—but my anti-pep talk isn't working today, and the customers haven't managed to knock my good mood out of me by the time Nico joins me for the last stint. I hand the customer his drink with a big grin and a "have a nice day!" and turn to see Nico smirking at me. "What?"

"You're in a good mood today."

I gasp with mock indignation. "I'm always in a good mood."

"Not true," he says with a raise of his brow and a smirk, "but even so." That makes me laugh.

"I just don't like early mornings," I insist, trying to explain away my frequent surly starts.

"Good to know." The tone that he says that in does something to me, but when I look back up at him, he's turned away as if nothing is wrong. There I go again, looking into things too much. It's him going out of his way to deliver me goodies yesterday—it's got my head all messed up. I blame the period hormones.

"Have you got any plans tonight?" I ask for something to say.

"I think I'm going to head to your gym. About time I actually put my money where my mouth is. Did you have any time tonight to show me the ropes?" Typical. The one time I get a chance to spend time with Nico that's not studying or working, and I have a date I'm excited about.

"Actually, I've got a date tonight," I start, intending to offer any other night, but my phone rings from the back. I must've forgotten to put it on silent. I grimace and head out to see who it is. Ezra. "Hello?"

"Hey, have you got a second?"

"Yeah," I reply, double-checking that no one is queueing.

"I'm running really late at the shop, we had a bit of a nightmare start. I'm not gonna make our reservation." See? Disappointment.

"Oh, that's okay. We'll reschedule."

"No way, we've already done that. Will you meet me at the shop when you're ready?" I agree because I don't want to wait for this either, and he gives me the address.

A couple of hours later, I'm coming up to the door of Vice Ink feeling unfamiliar butterflies in my stomach. Have I made too much of an effort? Not enough? I never second-guess things like this, but I'm nervous. I've gone with an off-white high-neck top with a floaty silver satin mini, my hair around my shoulders in waves, and I'm comfortable enough while still showing effort. My leather jacket and flat boots make it slightly more casual, too. I push my way through the door with a big exhale and pick Ezra out straight away past the counter, even if he is hunched over someone's back. There's a stunning girl at the front desk smiling at me, and I return her smile.

"You must be Harlow."

"Is it that obvious?" I must stick out like a sore thumb here.

"Not really, you grunge up well," she jokes. "You're as gorgeous as he said." I blush at the thought of Ezra telling people about me and decide I love this girl who's told me that. Maybe she can sense I'm nervous and need to hear it, or maybe she's just a lovely person. "Go on over," she says, gesturing to the back. "Ezra? Harlow's here."

As I step round the counter, I see the guy laying on his front as Ezra pauses and turns around to greet me with a smile.

"Fucking hell, Ezra," the guy says before either of us can say anything. I frown, but Ezra throws a punch to his arm.

"Keep your eyes off my girl." Ezra saying *my girl* has my insides warming.

"What, am I supposed to close my eyes around her? Jesus. You are well aware you're punching above your weight, right?" That makes me chuckle as Ezra glares some more at the poor guy.

"Do you mind if I look?" I ask the man.

"Not at all, sweetheart. Look all you want."

"I'm nearly finished," Ezra says. "This last bit shouldn't be too painful . . . unless he keeps flirting with you."

I take my chance to check out the tattoo as Ezra finishes. It's two figures locked in an embrace, taking up the guy's whole back—a woman, gorgeous and naked, and the Grim Reaper, complete with skull and hood. It looks like it could be a photo, it's that realistic, and I'm shocked at Ezra's talent.

"Oh my god, that's incredible," I breathe, and the guy looks up at me, grinning.

Ezra takes his gloves off and calls out to a younger guy hanging off to one side. "Arthur, can you help Jed with the mirror and wrap him so he can fuck off?" He nods and grabs supplies before heading over as Ezra grabs my hand and drags me into an office down a corridor at the back. I go to question our abrupt departure, but his lips are on mine before I can. He kisses me until I can't breathe, getting me hotter than any other kiss I've had without even touching me properly. "You look sensational," he murmurs against my lips, pulling back only far enough to get his words out.

"And that makes you . . . angry?"

"Not angry, territorial." I don't need to answer that, or to try and explain why that warms my stomach, because he's kissing me again, his mouth forceful against mine in a claiming kiss. We're both panting by the time we come up for air, and his hands are in my hair, cradling my head, his thumbs running along my jaw. "Sorry we missed our dinner reservation."

"That's okay," I whisper, my brain not completely back online after that kiss.

"I did something else. It's not the same, but will do for now, I hope."

He leads me further down the hallway, which opens up into a larger room around the corner. I can guess that it's normally a break room, but for now it has the table, chairs, and armchairs pushed to one side. Instead, there are cushions, pillows, and blankets in the middle, facing a projector screen. Fairy lights are strung everywhere around the room, giving it a romantic glow.

"Wow," I say articulately, emotion bubbling up at the thoughtfulness. "This is so . . . cute." His laugh bursts out of him.

"Okay, I deserve that," he says. "I know we could have done this at yours, but I wanted it to be a *date* date." I turn back to face him as my face splits with a huge grin.

"It's perfect. It's actually my *first* date date."

"Question one—how's it going so far?"

"It's going well," I say, pulling him toward me by his shirt and kissing him this time. I want to let him know how much this means to me. How he's the first guy I've wanted to actually date, and how happy I am that he still wanted to, even if sex is off the table tonight. He lets me lead, taking whatever I give him, but as I stroke his tongue with mine, he groans, and I pull back. "What's question two?"

"How on earth you got to twenty without going on a date."

"No one has your level of persistence," I joke, but he doesn't buy it for a second.

"I highly doubt that."

"I just don't date." I shrug.

"And yet here you are," he says, squeezing my waist in his hands.

"Looking for an ego stroke, are you?" That grin that seems to light up the room breaks free, and it's dazzling, as usual. I wonder how long it takes to get used to having Ezra's smile directed at you.

"No, I'm just curious. I'd be happy to know anything about you."

"There's really not much to know. I've never met anyone I felt like I wanted to spend more time with in that way."

"Never?" He looks at me like he can read my mind, and I really hope that's not true, because otherwise he'll know my mind went straight to Sawyer. I'd happily spend the rest of my days with Sawyer. I don't know how to answer, so I don't, and he lets me off the hook as someone knocks on the door.

"We're heading off, boss."

"Let me get everyone seen off and lock up," he says before dropping a light kiss to my lips and letting me go. "Make yourself comfy." He gives me a wink, and he's gone.

I do just that after he leaves and feel giddily happy as I shrug my jacket and toe my boots off, not wanting to stand on the nest Ezra has made with shoes on. When he comes back, I'm engrossed in the tablet left here, swiping through movies. I'm assuming it hooks up to the projector.

"Found one you like?"

"Not yet. You really thought of everything," I say as I look up at him and see the huge plate and glass bottle he's brought with him, along with two glasses.

"Hopefully," he replies as he takes his own boots off. "I wasn't sure what time you'd get here, so I thought cold food was better. But we can order something hot if you want?"

"No, this is fine! This is great." He sits down next to me and pulls my legs over his, eliminating the space between us before pouring us drinks. He's so casual with his touch, like it's completely natural for him, and I love it. It actually reminds me of how Sawyer is, but tonight is not for him. I put the tablet down without picking a movie and take a glass from Ezra.

"To perfect first dates," I offer as I hold my glass up.

"To perfect girls to plan them for," he adds, and we cheers before I struggle to drink with my smile.

"So you're pretty talented, huh?"

"Why do you sound so shocked?" he asks, but his face is jovial.

"Only because that tattoo was another level of stunning, not because I didn't think you were talented." Ezra shrugs, like it's not a big deal that he can create something like that with just his hands. "Is it just like tracing once the stencil is on there?" That gets a chuckle from him.

"I guess so, in a way. Have you got any tattoos?"

"Not yet." His eyebrows rise slightly at my vague answer.

"Oh? What have you got planned?" Now it's my turn to shrug. It's not that I don't want to tell him, but I can't tell if the whole situation will be awkward.

"Nothing major."

"It won't be a secret once it's on your skin."

"Depends where it is," I say coyly, taking a sip of my drink.

"I'd enjoy searching for it." His hand squeezes my thigh. "But you don't have to tell me. Tattoos can be personal, which needs trust." He lifts my legs off him before standing and offers me his hand. I take it without hesitation, but have to ask when he leads me back down the hallway.

"Where are we going?"

"To build trust," he says cryptically. I follow him out and he lifts me to sit on the end of the bench he was working at when I came in. Then he flits around, cleaning and sterilizing the space, and I'm content to watch him as I enjoy my bubbles. After a few minutes, he pulls a wheeled trolley over and sits on the bed facing me, his back against the rest.

"What's going on?"

He doesn't answer, just pulls his top off, and my eyes roam eagerly over his torso. He is beautiful. His muscles are defined through his rich skin, and he's covered in tattoos. The sleeve that I've only seen once or twice reaches up and over his shoulder and bleeds onto his chest and stomach. Maybe he should only wear short sleeves from now on? That would've made it easier to tell him apart from Eli. My stomach roils at the memories of Eli, but I push them down and focus back on Ezra's tattoos. They seem like lots of separate tattoos instead of one large piece, but each is a mini masterpiece. He sticks something onto his side, and when he peels it away, my mouth hangs open. Outlined in a bright purple is the famous Barbie-head silhouette. I lift my hand up to touch it, but Ezra gently takes my wrist.

"It won't be dry yet."

"You can't be serious," I say, dumbfounded, as I lean forward to take a closer look. I don't know if I expect it to change suddenly and not be some kind of ode to me, but nope, it's still the same.

"I am serious."

"You do know this is permanent, right?" My brain finally gets around to the other huge issue here.

"As a tattoo artist, I'm aware of that, thank you." He huffs a laugh.

"But like, *on your skin* permanent."

"You're already under my skin. May as well be on it too."

Wow. Okay, that was smooth. I grin, and he matches me before cupping my cheek and giving me a light kiss. "But—"

"Harlow, stop stressing. Tattoos are like a scrap book for me. This doesn't mean you have to marry me, it's fun for me."

"Okay," I say disbelievingly, because he's crazy. But he's also an adult and can make his own decisions, I guess. At least it's not my name across his heart or anything. "Can you tattoo yourself?" I ask, tamping down the urge to convince him not to do this.

"I could . . . but you're going to do it." I snap my head up to look at him instead of the tattoo stencil.

"Ah, no I'm not!"

"Of course you are. You're not scared of needles, are you?"

"I'm not scared, but these are gorgeous. Whoever did these will not be happy I'm messing up their artwork."

"I don't mind," he says smugly.

"You did these?!"

"I drew them, but I didn't tattoo them on. Come on."

"But—"

"No buts," he insists as he pulls my legs over and his up so they're straight on the bench. I wind up straddling him, giving me a great view of the tattoo. "I trust you," he says before he hands me the gun, and I steel myself to actually do this. Clearly, he's a determined guy.

"Fine. But no moaning when I mess up."

"I just want you to do a couple of token lines. If your hand is steady enough, you can do the whole outline." I nod and he starts the gun up. It's not as hard as I was expecting, especially with Ezra there coaching me through. Not that it looks anywhere near as good as his work, but the few lines I complete are okay.

"Right, that's it," Ezra says. "I think we're pushing our luck now. We're at the part where someone needs to take over." He takes the gun from me, switching it off and placing it back on the trolley. "You did great."

"You haven't even seen it."

"Yeah, but I'm pretty sure you didn't give me blood poisoning, which for your first time straight onto skin is impressive." I gape at him, trying to decide if he's joking or not.

"That was a possibility?!"

"Come on," he says, lifting me down instead of answering and standing up with me. "I'll clean this, and then we can eat and you can let me sketch your design."

And that's what we do. It's surprisingly easy to let Ezra into my thoughts, and as he shows me different versions of my very first tattoo design, I marvel at how easily he slips into my head *and* my heart.

Chapter 14

Nico

"You're in a bad mood today," Fleur very unhelpfully comments at my obvious sour mood. I shrug, because I know whatever I say will be reported back to Harlow, so I can't exactly sulk out loud about how she's found someone else. *Fuck.* I can't believe it. Well, I can—it's Harlow, it was going to happen eventually—but I'm gutted. I can't believe I'm too late. I should've told her. But no, I shouldn't have. What I'm doing is right. And maybe her and Ezra won't last anyway. It was just a date. Her first date.

"I guess this isn't a great time to ask, then, but do you mind if I shoot off?" She looks apologetic, but it's fine. We cover for each other all the time, and it's quiet now that we're so close to the end of opening hours.

"No, of course not."

I carry on clearing up and am changing over the dishwasher in the back when the bell rings, signaling a customer. Heading out, I'm expecting a late commuter, but Harlow is making her way to the counter, looking around the empty shop. She looks phenomenal, and even though the clothes she normally wears are formfitting, the gym kit she's got on now is like a second skin.

"Hey. Is Fleur not here?" she asks.

"No, she shot off early. We've been quiet."

"Oh, okay. Just a coffee then, please."

"On the way?" I ask, gesturing to the bag she's holding.

"Just finished, hence the sweaty mess." That couldn't be further from the truth, and suddenly, I don't want to go back to my apartment alone. Even if I can't have her like that, I still want to be around her. I always have.

"Want a study session?" Her eyebrows rise at my sudden offer.

"Yeah, I would love that. Let me help you close up, then."

We work in companionable silence while we shut up shop, and I make us both a drink to take with us. I have enough notes with me to produce a session as I had class earlier, and Harlow wants to shower, so we decide to hold it at her place.

I've never actually been inside before, but it's cozy and inviting. I set up on the island while she has a shower. Hearing it and knowing she's one door away, naked and dripping, is the worst form of torture. She finally ends my torment and joins me in a tank and sweats, damp hair in a messy bun, and I'm stunned again by how naturally gorgeous she is. Those big blue eyes, fluttery eyelashes, and pouty lips—I know she hates the Barbie reference, but she is the epitome of a model doll.

Just as we're getting started, there's a short, sharp knock on the door, and it swings open before Harlow can stand. Ezra blows out a breath as his eyes land on her.

"What?" she asks, startled at his relief.

"I was checking you got home okay. You're not answering your phone." He comes to stand beside me with his phone in his hand. I don't mean to look, but the screen pulls my attention. It's got what looks like a weird game of Pac-Man on it.

"It's in my gym bag, still on silent," she explains. "Is everything okay?"

"Yeah. The Guards are out nearby, and I wanted to make sure you weren't out there still."

"What do you mean 'out'?" I ask, and he pulls his phone closer to his chest when he realizes I can see. "How do you know that?"

"It's all over social media. They've already beaten the living shit out of two random guys."

"What? It's not even dark."

"I know. They're getting more brazen."

"They never come here, though."

"They're not. They're over by Springhill, but who knows where they'll end up."

"What? That's by you!" Harlow declares, spinning her focus to me.

"Yeah. Hopefully they'll move on soon."

Ezra glances down at his phone, and his mouth tightens, but he doesn't say anything as he gives me a doubtful look. "Hopefully." What is on that thing?

"Wait, Sawyer's out still," Harlow says in a panic, rifling through her gym bag.

"Where?"

"I'm not sure. He was going to meet someone after work." She dials on her phone and has it to her ear by the time she's finished speaking. We're all quiet while it rings, and he answers after what feels like an eternity. "Sawyer! Where are you?" A frown settles on her face, and I want to reach out and smooth it away. "You keep cutting out. Sawyer? Sawyer?" She pulls the phone away and groans. "Dammit. The signal is rubbish."

"Send him a message. It might be easier to get through than holding a full call, or he might have wi-fi."

Harlow: **Where are you?**

We wait. Harlow chews on her lip nervously as we wait for some update on what's happening. She gasps when a reply comes through.

Sawyer: **Just leaving Kevin's. Everything okay?**

"Shit, shit, shit. Kevin lives in Springhill. What are we going to do?" Her eyes are flicking between Ezra and I, and her chest is picking up speed as she takes shallow breaths, on the way to a full freak-out. That's a side of Harlow I've not seen before, and I'll do anything to help her calm down. Ezra grabs her phone and messages him back as we both watch.

Harlow: **Stay there**

Sawyer: **I've already left. What's going on?**

Harlow: **The Guards are out there**

Sawyer: **I'm on my way back**

"I don't like him being there at all," Harlow argues.

"I'll go and get him," I offer, wanting to help in some way. I really, really shouldn't, and my father would rip me a new one if I was seen. There's very good reasons why I'm supposed to be staying under the radar. But I want to help, and I am used to that area.

"No way."

"I need to go back there anyway," I reason with Harlow. "I live there."

"Maybe they've gone?" she asks hopefully.

"They haven't." How does Ezra know that? What is that "game"?

"I'll come with you," he says. "We'll avoid them."

"How will we do that?"

"Just trust me," he declares confidently, and I find myself trusting him.

"Let me get my shoes on," Harlow starts, but Ezra holds her still by her shoulders.

"You're not coming."

"What?!" Harlow goes to knock his hands off her, but he grabs her shoulders again and leans in close.

"I'm not taking you into danger."

"But you're both going!"

"Yeah, to get Sawyer, so we know he's safe and you can relax. You either stay here, or we don't go." His voice is soft, even if it remains determined. Harlow chews her lip with a furrow in her brow while she considers her options. Eventually, she caves.

"Fine. I'll stay here. Can you keep me updated?"

"Of course. You ready?" Ezra asks me, and I shake my keys to show I am. My car is just out front, and he gives a low whistle when he sees it.

"Coffee shop pay well, does it?" I don't answer, and I pull away as soon as we're both seated. Ezra remains glued to his phone, and my curiosity wins out.

"What have you got there?"

"My phone," he says simply.

"Oh, come on. Is it Hunt-A-Guard or something? It's obvious you know more than you're letting on." Out of the corner of my eye, I can see him eyeing me warily, but I keep my focus on the road.

"More like Avoid-A-Guard," he eventually says.

"How did you manage to get that?" I've never heard of software like that being created, not to mention the illegality of tracking people without their knowledge, and I'm sure if my father had, he'd have it by now.

"I made it. It wasn't hard."

"For you, or in general? Because I'm pretty sure it would be hard for anyone else." What secret talents is Ezra hiding?

"You're very inquisitive," he says instead of answering, but I'm not put off.

"From what I gather, that app you've made is tracking the Guards, whether it's to avoid them or not. You can't have bugged them all physically, so I'm guessing you've hacked into something—maybe the telecommunications network? And anyway, how can you be sure you've got them all?"

"I've got them all."

"How do you know? It's not like they keep a payroll and report income to the tax department. Either you've bugged each and every one of them—not likely, because it'd have to be undetectable on scanners and wouldn't account for new gang members—or you somehow have a list of them and are tracking every single phone of anyone affiliated with the Guards. Not only would that be illegal, but it would have to be undetectable to their own hackers. You couldn't leave a trail of breadcrumbs that could lead back to you. So, what are you? Law enforcement?" Ezra definitely has some secret talents. I wonder if they're a secret to Harlow too?

"You know a lot about technology."

"I know a lot about the premise, I wouldn't have a clue about how to execute it. Criminology is more my forte."

"Good to know," he comments lightly, but I have the feeling he's filing away that bit of information. He also hasn't answered my question. "And you're right. It is nearly impossible. But not completely. Turn left."

His abrupt direction takes me aback, but I follow it, even if it's heading the wrong way, assuming it's to avoid Guards. We don't talk any more. Ezra is focused on the app and giving more directions until we pull up outside an apartment block a couple roads over from mine. Ezra messages Sawyer and Harlow to say we're outside, and it's not long before Sawyer is joining us.

"Thanks for this, guys. I was happy to wait it out."

"Harlow was worried about you," I say, and he nods. I'm sure he'd do whatever it takes for her to be happy, just like any of us would. We hear about another three people attacked as we're on the way back, and I think we're all glad when we pull up outside their apartment block. By the time I'm inside after Sawyer and Ezra, Harlow has jumped up and wrapped herself around Sawyer in a giant hug. His arms cradle her back, and relief flashes across her face as she looks over his shoulder and sees us.

"We have to be ready, Sawyer," she says, her eyes flitting between Ezra and I.

"We will be, Angel." He sets her down and gives her a kiss on the top of her head.

Harlow turns to hug Ezra, then surprises me by hugging me too, and I squeeze her tight. I can always use the excuse of adrenaline later.

"Have you eaten?" Sawyer asks Harlow, and she shakes her head. "I'll order some dinner. Ezra, you staying?"

"Yep," he replies, pulling Harlow back into his arms and giving her a light kiss. I start to pack my stuff up, assuming Harlow isn't in the right headspace for studying.

"You're not veggie or anything, Nico?" Sawyer asks.

"No, but I should get back before it's too dark. Thanks anyway, man."

"Don't go!" Harlow blurts, pulling stiffly out of Ezra's embrace. "Stay here, just for the night. Just until we know they're gone. Unless you have to get back for your girlfriend or something? But I'm sure she'd understand you not heading back on your own when they're so crazy right now." She's babbling, and when I look to Ezra and Sawyer for an opinion, they both shrug. "The sofa's pretty comfy, or—"

"Okay, I'll stay," I say with a smile before she talks herself out of the invite or stresses even more.

"I didn't realize you could say so many words at once, Angel," Sawyer mocks, and she rolls her eyes, but the atmosphere is light again. Harlow settles as Ezra winds his arms around her from behind and leans down so his mouth is by her ear.

"Do I get a sleepover invitation that enthusiastic?" Harlow blushes and flicks her eyes up to mine to see if I've heard. I smirk at her.

"You're all annoying," she says with a mock huff as she pulls out of Ezra's hold and heads for the sofa. "Sawyer, are you feeding us or what?"

"Yes, ma'am."

Chapter 15

Harlow

I'm bleary-eyed as I let myself back into the apartment after my morning shift. Nico offered to cover for me, but it's his first day off in weeks and he didn't even get to stay at his own place last night, so I refused. The sofa is empty, so I assume he's gone home now that the coast is clear, and disappointment settles inside me. I head to Sawyer's room instead, hoping the comfortable atmosphere from yesterday is still holding after our awkward couple of days, but as I open the door ready to say something, I freeze with my mouth open. Nico and Sawyer. Half-naked. *Both* half-naked. Both now staring at me as I impersonate a guppy fish. Could I be any less smooth?

"Shit, sorry. I didn't realize you were here."

"It's fine," Sawyer replies as his eyebrows crease. "I'm just lending Nico a fresh shirt."

"Okay," I say, pulling the door shut as I leave completely and utterly flustered. I'm downing a glass of water and have managed to compose myself somewhat when they come out.

"Do you want to get breakfast? We were waiting for you to get back, and I'm showing Nico the gym after."

"Sounds good."

"Go grab Ezra. He usually works lates, so he should be home."

He is, and it ends up with all four of us going to eat. I love that Sawyer automatically includes Ezra, and now that everyone is fully clothed, I'm able to be myself and relax. I was worried that last night might've been a fluke because of the adrenaline, but they all still get on so easily this morning too. Contentment overwhelms me, having all of them close, and I'm happy to chill with them all. Except when Ezra touches me, which is a lot. Then my brain does a weird short-circuit thing, and I become very aware that my period has finished and it's been *way* too long since I've had sex.

We go to a new diner, and the waitress's eyes light up when she comes to take our order. Possessiveness builds up inside me so fiercely I have to fist my hands under the table, which is ridiculous, because none of these guys are mine. Ezra and I haven't talked about being exclusive, although tattooing his skin is pretty symbolic. Sawyer gets more than enough action to prove he doesn't belong to me, and Nico has an actual girlfriend who isn't me. Even knowing this logically, I want to throat punch the woman as she flutters her eyelashes at them all.

Nico and Sawyer order first, sitting opposite us, and Ezra throws an arm over my shoulders, pulling me toward him to kiss the side of my head. I love the obvious sign he's with me in the face of her flirting, and I look up at him with grateful eyes.

"Stop looking at me like that." Of all the sentences that come out of his mouth, that one may be my favorite. So far, at least.

"Like what?" The waitress clears her throat before he can answer, and when I turn to her, I realize that she's waiting for our orders . . . along with Nico and Sawyer, who are watching us. Awkward.

"Sorry." My cheeks redden at getting caught. "I'll have the veggie scramble with bacon and a vanilla shake, please." Ezra chuckles and orders for himself while I avoid everyone's gaze.

"How was work this morning?" Nico asks when the waitress collects our menus and leaves.

"Not too bad. What have you lot been up to?"

"I'd only just pulled myself together when you got back."

"I spoke to my mum," Sawyer adds, and I perk up. I adore Sawyer's parents. I spent every minute I could at their house when I was younger and relished in the dynamics of a proper, loving family. They have such a warm, inviting aura, and they were happy for me to entertain Sawyer. Being an only child full of energy, he was a full-on kid. I'm sure the pact between us was a weight off their minds as we grew up.

"Oh, yeah? How are they doing?"

"Good. Dad's having a great week."

"That's amazing, I'm glad to hear it."

"He asked if we could visit this afternoon, but I've got back-to-back PT clients booked in."

"I'm working too," I say, my heart heavy.

"I can cover for you," Nico offers.

"Thanks, but Sawyer's busy anyway." That's a shame, and awful timing. We've not been invited very often since the attack. It affected his dad's mental state more than it affected him physically, and that's saying something.

"You should still go. You know you're his favorite anyway," Sawyer teases.

"Are you sure?"

"Of course. Why don't you introduce them to Ezra? Might cheer him up."

"To know I actually have a heart?"

"Something like that," he agrees, but his smile doesn't quite reach his eyes. "Two o'clock, they said, and I don't want you getting home alone."

"I'm really sorry, I can't go," Ezra says. "I've got a late start today and it's too short notice to reschedule my clients."

"That's fine," I quickly reassure him. I shouldn't have gotten so ahead of myself without checking. "I should wait for Sawyer anyway." I'm gutted, having no idea when his father will be feeling up to it again. The waitress brings our drinks over, and Nico is engrossed in his phone while we pass them round.

"I'll take you," Nico says as I take a long sip of my milkshake.

"Huh?"

"To Sawyer's parents' place." I frown slightly. How can he cover my shift and drive me there?

"I still have work."

"Celeste is going to cover."

"Since when?"

"Since I asked her to."

"But—"

"Harlow, it's done. Just say okay," he smiles. "You clearly want to go, and I want to say thanks for having me stay."

"You mean forcing you to sleep on my sofa."

"Same thing," he says, smile growing.

"Are you sure?" I know it's a lot, but he is offering, and I really do want to go.

"Yep."

"Are you sure you don't mind?" I double-check with Sawyer.

"Of course not. You're family. You've seen my parents loads of times alone."

"I know." I also know he'll be gutted to miss out. The food arrives, and we chat easily before we're getting ready to leave. I excuse myself to the toilet before our drive, and as I'm on my way back, someone spins away from the counter to face me as I head toward them.

"Hey, sweetheart." I smile politely without replying and go to walk around him, but he stands up off his stool to block my way. The distinctive sound of chairs scraping against the floor comes from behind him, but he doesn't seem to notice or register why.

"Can I buy you—"

"No." He spins to face whoever answered and comes face-to-face with a simmering Ezra.

"I didn't even finish my sentence."

"Doesn't matter, the answer is no." The guy thankfully holds his hands up and sits back onto his stool.

"Alright, I didn't realize she was spoken for. Protective one there, love," he says to me. "Or do they come as a pack?" For the first time, I notice the other two standing further back, waiting to back Ezra, and my chest warms at their bromance. Nico fits in with them both so easily, and they're already ready to protect each other. Plus, they even *look* good together. Individually, they'd easily be any girl's fantasy. Together, they are undoubtedly mine.

Chapter 16

Nico

WE HEAD BACK TO the car, and I drop Ezra at the shop and Sawyer at the gym before Harlow and I set off for her visit. I have so much studying I could be doing today, but I'll take any chance to spend more time with Harlow, especially if it makes her this happy. She's practically vibrating in her seat.

"You're excited," I say, taking in her happy glow.

"Yeah," she agrees, and her grin somehow grows even bigger. She's so fucking beautiful.

"How long's it been since you saw them?"

"A month or so." That surprises me—it doesn't seem like an overly long time.

"I know what you're thinking," she says. "That's not a long time."

That is exactly what I'm thinking, but I shrug. "Depends, I guess."

"On?"

"Whether you like your parents. Or your friends' parents."

"Do you like yours?" she asks, turning to face me in her seat.

"Weren't we talking about you?" I can't give her my undivided attention, with having to watch the road, but she's giving me hers.

"I'm not so interesting," she says.

"I beg to differ." I can feel her eyes on me, searching for something.

"I do like them . . . my *friend's* parents. They practically brought me up. Their house was my safe space, my escape." Escape from what? I don't want her to feel like I'm interrogating her and close down, so I try to ease in to getting more details.

"Why don't you see them more now?" She takes a moment before she answers, and it's a careful response.

"Callen doesn't like to see people sometimes."

"Why's that?"

"You'll see." That seems like the end of that avenue, so I try another one.

"How often do you see your own parents?" I know I'm prying, but I want to know everything about her. She chuckles, but there's no humor in it, and she silently turns back in her seat to face the front. Wrong avenue.

"I'm gonna need to be a lot less sober to have that conversation."

"But we will have it?" I ask, grasping on to the fact that she's not shutting me down because she doesn't trust me with the information, just that it might be hard for her to give it.

"Yeah. When you're ready to feel depressed, let me know."

"Okay." And I know I will. I'm desperate for any scrap of Harlow, past or present. She's lost in thought for a moment before turning back to me.

"Are we talking about you now?" she asks.

"What do you want to know?" Fair is fair, but it seems Harlow is over the deep confessions.

"What's your favorite car karaoke song?" That makes me laugh, and I tell her and spend the rest of the journey being entertained by her enthusiastic renditions.

We finally pull up to their house, and I know why Sawyer didn't want her to come here alone. We're in prime Guard territory, and even being here in broad daylight makes me edgy. Harlow doesn't seem to be affected, though, jumping out of the car and running to the door. She knocks lighter than her pent-up excitement suggests, and I've just caught up to her when the door opens and she throws herself at the small woman inside.

"Pearl," she squeals, holding the woman tightly.

"Harlow," the woman replies warmly. "It's so lovely to see you! And who's this?" she asks over Harlow's shoulder. Harlow pulls back and steps aside.

"This is Nico. He . . ." She looks over to me like she's not sure how to introduce me but settles on, "We work together."

"Well, hello, Nico. Come in, both of you. Callen's excited to see you."

We follow her into a sitting room, and Harlow is in the arms of a man in a wheelchair before either of them even speak.

"Harlow, my love," he murmurs as they hold each other for a minute. "It's so good to see you." She stands up again, and he looks over to me. "Hi, son." It's clearly meant as a welcome greeting, and it's kind of jarring to hear it with warmth rather than in a taunt. More jarring than the scars covering his head.

"Hi, sir. It's lovely to meet you both."

"He didn't even flinch. Where did you find him, Harlow?"

She rolls her eyes. "You're not Quasimodo, Callen. I keep telling you that."

"Nico works with Harlow," Pearl explains to her husband.

"He gave me a lift," Harlow adds. "Sawyer is gutted he can't be here."

"We know. We'll see him another time. Take a seat, both of you. What's going on?"

"Literally nothing," Harlow replies as we sit next to each other on the sofa and Pearl perches on the arm of Callen's chair.

"Oh, really? Because I think you're keeping something from us." Harlow's face goes white. "Sawyer mentioned you've finally taken a fancy to someone."

"Oh." She breathes out in relief. What did she think Pearl was going to say? "I guess so. Maybe."

"And it's not this hunk?" Callen jokes, gesturing to me. "The other guy must really be something."

"Callen, don't embarrass her," Pearl chides half-heartedly.

"His name is Ezra, and Sawyer shouldn't have mentioned anything. It's still new."

"You'll bring him next time," Callen says without a hint of question in his voice, and Harlow sighs.

"Fine. If he hasn't gotten sick of me by then, I'll bring him." I'm pretty sure she's joking, or at least pretending to, but Callen frowns.

"You are perfect, dear girl. Anyone would be lucky to be given the chance to woo you. Don't ever forget that."

"Thanks, Callen." I get the feeling he's told her that many times, but it still seems to mean a lot to her.

"Tea, anyone?"

"Let me help." Pearl says it's not necessary, but I insist as I stand to follow her out.

"Well then, I won't say no to a strapping young man in the kitchen."

"Keep your hands off my wife," Callen objects playfully as we leave.

"Thanks for bringing her," Pearl says when we're alone in the kitchen. "He loves to see her."

"Of course."

"You like her, huh?" That takes me off guard.

"Uh . . ."

"It's okay, you don't need to spill your secrets to this old lady. I know the way a smitten man looks at his woman, and I'm not surprised. She's something special."

"She is." I don't know what else to say, so I leave it at that.

"She's so good for Callen, her and Sawyer both."

"They seem really close." She smiles as she moves around the kitchen, boiling the kettle and gathering cups.

"They are. He's been like a father to her, and she's his daughter, in his eyes. I think he's still kind of hoping they might end up together." Harlow and Sawyer? I'm not brave enough to ask, but I'm pretty sure I know the answer. "Some days, it's probably all that keeps him going." We're quiet while she arranges the tray. "Are you going to ask?"

There's a moment of silence before I say, "It's none of my business." I don't want her to think I'm digging for gossip.

"Maybe not, but it really means a lot that you brought her. He's had good days and bad days since the brain injury. She'd have been gutted to miss him asking for her, and he'd have been gutted to have missed her on a good day."

"Any time. I can bring her around any time." And I mean it. Anything to see Harlow so happy and comfortable.

I carry the tray in, and we sit and have tea while Callen recalls tales from Harlow and Sawyer's younger days. She pretends to be embarrassed, but as she laughs and chats with them, I can see how over the moon she is. He's also obviously still so in love with his wife, and by all appearances, the feeling's mutual. It's unusual and lovely in equal measure to be around such unapologetic, comfortable love.

It's a few hours before we leave to head home, and Harlow is quiet on the way back.

"Are you okay?" I ask after a while, unsure if she wants an excuse to talk or not.

"Yeah. Thank y—"

"Believe me," I chuckle. "I've been thanked enough today. And you're very welcome." She's chewing on her lip, and I think she's going to go quiet again.

"He got jumped," she says. Damn. There's always the chance that it was a car accident or something, but I was wondering, given where they live.

"By the Guards?"

"By the Seconds." My blood runs cold, and my hands tighten around the steering wheel. Lost in the past, she doesn't seem to notice, thankfully. "He was in the wrong place at the wrong time, and they assumed he was a Guard. He was never involved in anything like that, but something big had happened and there was a lot of violence that night. He nearly died." It's an effort to keep my breathing even, and I swallow harshly. "He's paralyzed from the waist down and has trouble with his motor skills sometimes, as well as the brain injury . . . it caused some personality changes. Sometimes anger issues. It's affected his mental health, and he won't see us if he's feeling worthless, useless. Not like the person he used to be. He was everything to all three of us when we were growing up, and he's still adjusting to being a different form of supportive, I guess."

"How long has it been?"

"Two years. Just after the last Games." I knew the violence she was talking about. I knew who had ordered it, and why it was happening. My chest is tight and my vision tunnels, but I can't let her see my reaction. I try to take quiet deep breaths and compose myself.

"Is he getting the support he can?" I'll make sure he is. Somehow, however I can, I have to find a way to atone for this.

"Yeah, he is. It's an ongoing struggle." Harlow slips back into thought, and I try not to release my rage. At this moment, I hate everything I am. Everything I was brought up with, everything I try to stay away from.

As we pull up in front of her apartment, Harlow unclips her seatbelt.

"Thanks so much." The fact that she's thanking me—that Pearl and Callen thanked me, hosted me, after all they've been through—makes me nauseous.

"No worries," I say, too crippled by emotion to say anything else.

"Do you want to come in?"

"No. I should get going." Her brow furrows at my sharp tone, but I'm only just holding it together. I need to get out of here, and away from her, before I lose it.

"Be careful. Okay?" The look of concern in her eyes breaks my heart, but I have to go.

"I'll be fine. Goodbye, Harlow."

"Bye, Nico."

I need to make that goodbye permanent before it's too hard to let her go.

Chapter 17

Harlow

Fleur joins me in the afternoon, taking over from Celeste. Nico isn't at work today, and I feel kind of odd about how we left off yesterday. I don't know if he was just tired after sleeping on the sofa, or if we were out longer than he expected to be, but he definitely seemed off.

"Since when does Nico get your shifts covered?" Fleur asks as soon as my customer leaves the counter.

"Since he got stuck at mine overnight when the Guards were out in his area."

"Oh my god, I didn't realize he lived that far out."

"Yeah, pretty much right in the worst of it," I say, trying to hide my wince. I hate that he's so close to all of the shit that goes down. We were lucky he was at mine when Ezra came in.

"Oh, shit. But he's fine?"

"Yeah, absolutely fine."

"Good. So let's circle back to the fact that you had a sleepover with him," she says, shaking my arm in excitement. Fleur is well aware of my crush on Nico.

"I didn't have a *sleepover* with him. He stayed on the sofa."

"And nothing happened?" she asks disappointedly.

"No. He has a girlfriend, remember? We saw her with him."

"I notice that you're not saying anything about *you* being taken. Things not going well with Ezra?"

"Things are going great. It's still early days, though."

Fleur sighs. "And you're allergic to commitment. You know, I could see you seeing more than one person, rocking the casual life," she muses, and I shrug as I sip on my drink. I'm not adverse to seeing Ezra and Nico at the same time, but not because I think it'll be casual. Ezra's comments at the party really got me thinking. I've never wanted more than one partner before, but I've never had this crazy attraction to anyone before either. Even though Sawyer and Nico are both unavailable, they still feel like they should be mine.

"Do you want to do something tonight?" Fleur asks. "I could do with some girl time."

"Of course. You can let me know how Lee has been."

"He's been the same. I don't think he's cheating on me, but he's definitely hiding something. Maybe I'm just being naive." Fleur was sickeningly happy with Lee before all this happened, so it's a shame he's making her question their relationship right now. I want to shake him and remind him how amazing his girlfriend is.

"I'd trust your instincts," I say. "They're usually spot on."

"Like how I knew you liked Ezra?" she asks with a wiggle of her brows, and I smile.

"Aren't we talking about you?"

"Nah," she says with a smile, and I let her drop it. Until later, anyway. "Yours tonight, then?"

"How about dinner?" I suggest. "We can go to that outdoor Mexican place."

She agrees, and we head there straight from work since the restaurant has such a casual vibe. We order sharing platters and a margarita each and indulge in some good old girl time. When she pops to the toilet, I check my phone and reply to some messages, leaving the two from Ezra for last.

Ezra: **Hey gorgeous, are you free tonight?**

Ezra: **I'm assuming this means no, but maybe you'll have read my mind and be waiting in my bed when I get home.**

"What are you grinning at?"

"Sorry," I say as Fleur makes me jump. "It's Ezra."

"Don't apologize. It's great to see you excited over a guy."

"It's weird, huh?" It feels weird to me. I haven't had to confront my feelings for a guy before, there's always been a reason to not be open about how I feel about Nico, and

Sawyer is so different to "like." Spotting someone I'm mildly attracted to in a club doesn't count.

"Yeah, but in a good way," Fleur agrees. "You deserve someone to get excited about. Are you seeing him tonight?"

"I don't know. I'm kind of nervous," I admit.

"You?! Why?"

I decide to just spit out what I'm thinking about. If you can't be honest with your best friend, who can you be honest with?

"What if the sex is shit like with everyone else?"

She gives me a look full of sympathy. "Why would it be? He makes you feel different to everyone else."

Not everyone. "I guess." I down the last of my margarita.

"Come on," she says, doing a little dance in her seat, "get your Porno Barbie vibes on." I glare as she chuckles at me. Definitely should not have told her that story. She laughs. "I'm just winding you up, but honestly, you're hot as fuck and so is he. You need to test the sex out ASAP."

"You're right," I say, feeling Fleur's optimism and maybe a little liquid courage take over. I pull out my phone.

Harlow: **Not yours, mine**

Ezra: **How am I supposed to concentrate on work now?**

"Well, I've definitely lost your focus," Fleur says, but she's grinning when I look back up.

"Sorry."

"Don't be. Let's go, but I want all the details!"

I spend the whole walk home engrossed in my phone and getting more excited to see Ezra. Fleur's right, this is my forte, and honestly, I think sex is important in a relationship. I need to know what I'm working with from the beginning. No one has ever bothered to make me come during sex before, but that doesn't mean it's all been *bad*. Actually . . . yeah, it does. But that doesn't mean that all sex will be bad, just that the guys who want quick club hookups aren't necessarily interested in making it good for the other person. I at least know that pleasure is possible because I take matters into my own hands just fine. The issue is finding a guy that bothers to *try*.

I message Ezra to let him know I'm home, but he doesn't reply instantly, so I assume he's gone back to tattooing and jump in the shower. I'm on my way back to my room when the front door opens quickly and slams shut again, making me spin toward it. Ezra marches toward me, clasps my face with his hands and crashes his lips against mine before I can even say hi. He's as eager for this as I am, then. Good to know. He walks me slowly backward into my room and kicks the door shut behind him as I slide my hands under his shirt, tracing the muscles in his stomach. As he pulls back slightly, I take the chance to pull his shirt off, and he grins at my enthusiasm.

"Hi," he says.

"Hi," I say back, grinning. I spot the little square of cling film taped to his abs, showing his new tattoo. "You got it finished."

"Yep. Told you I'd be proud to have you at my side." He wraps his arms around me, and I loop mine around his neck, pulling him down to kiss me again. He lifts me, walking back toward the bed before lowering us both so he's hovering above me on his forearms, his hips settled between my thighs.

"You really couldn't concentrate on work, huh?" I ask.

"Definitely not, but I was done with clients anyway. I was messing around with your stencil. Can't wait to see it on you." I'm so excited to get it and glad that he pushed me to take the leap, even knowing that it's for another guy. He gets and accepts my friendship with Sawyer, no questions asked. After undoing his trousers, I snake my hand between us and wrap it around his length, but he pulls my hand away before I can have any real fun.

"Wait," he whispers. "I need to see you." He sits back on his feet and undoes my towel, pushing it open so it falls to the sides. I'm not shy about my body at all, and seeing his gaze darken as he takes me in warms my skin. I give him a small smile.

"Fuck, Harlow," he breathes, rubbing a hand down his face.

"Yes, fuck Harlow," I agree, reaching out to grab at him, but he dodges my hands with a low chuckle.

"Oh, I intend to." He gently traces his fingertips around the swell of my breast and then my nipple before pinching it lightly. With hooded eyes, he looks up at my slight gasp. Lowering himself again, he takes my sensitive nipple into his mouth, sucking lightly as he traces the other, and if I could rub my thighs together, I'd be golden. Instead, I arch my back so that my breast presses to his mouth, wordlessly begging for more. He lets my nipple go with a pop, his teeth gently scraping the underside, and my legs tighten around him.

"Ezra," I breathe, desperate for *more.* He doesn't reply but runs his thumb over the bundle of nerves between my thighs, and I dig my fingers into the mattress, gripping handfuls of sheet. Moving lower, he puts a pillow under my hips and then places my legs over his shoulders, moving his hungry gaze from my face to between my legs.

He lowers himself onto his forearms and inhales deeply, making my stomach clench as he growls. Leaning in, he swirls his tongue around my clit in one torturously slow circle. I buck off the bed, willing him to stay right where he is, but he presses a hand to my lower stomach to still me as he trails his tongue leisurely from clit to entrance. I barely breathe while I wait for his next move to bring me pleasure, and it does—shallowly fucking me with his tongue until I'm quivering and squirming, desperate for more. "Ezra, please," I moan, and he groans.

"That's like music to my ears," he says, plunging two fingers inside me to replace his tongue, putting it to better use against my clit, and I detonate as he sucks my clit while curling the fingers pumping inside me. I writhe as pleasure saturates my limbs, and all I can do is try to catch my breath and blink at him as he crawls back over me.

"You're pretty good at that, huh?" I finally manage to say.

He huffs a laugh. "You haven't seen anything yet." Leaning over me, he takes my lips in an eager kiss, and the taste of myself on his tongue has me wrapping my legs around his waist. I pull him toward me, inching his hips closer until I feel the head of his cock pressing against my entrance, but he's holding back.

He breathes against my lips, "Harlow, I—" but I'm done waiting.

"Ezra, I need you. *Please.*" He must hear the need in my voice because he groans, and the feel of his cock penetrating me obliterates any other thought I might have. The friction of him pulling out and pushing in again until he's fully seated is exquisite, and it causes tremors to run through my body.

"Fuck, you feel incredible," he breathes as he rotates his hips, causing me to moan as he rubs against my swollen clit. "Open your eyes, Harlow." I blink them open to see him looking down at me with so much lust in his eyes I clench around him, and he groans.

Leaning on a forearm with his other arm above my head, he starts to pump his hips, and I feel so cherished and so full and suddenly completely overwhelmed. Pushing the thoughts out of my head, I pull his hips down and focus on the pleasure erupting inside me. He picks up speed, pistoning in and out of me, and I build again quickly, pleasure blinding me as his pelvis grinds against my clit with every thrust. He massages my breast and then pinches my nipple, pulling it slightly harder than before, which pushes me over the edge into another orgasm, this one hitting me with the intensity of a high-speed train. Ezra buries his head into my shoulder and bites down with a muffled growl as he pushes somehow deeper, feeling impossibly deep, before finishing inside me.

When I've centered myself again and pry my eyes open, he's looking down at me with pure adoration. It hits me straight in the chest as I meet his gaze, and his brow pinches.

"You okay?"

"Yeah," I manage to get out, and I pull him down for a kiss so I don't have to look at him. When he gently pulls out of me, I push him to the side and quickly stand.

"Harlow," he starts, but I'm already halfway to the door.

"I'm just going to get cleaned up," I say.

"Let me—"

But I'm gone, and I don't even think to get dressed first. Thankfully, Sawyer is god knows where. Shutting the bathroom door, I lock it behind me, but a knock comes right after.

"Harlow, what's going on?" What a good question. What is going on? *Well, Ezra, I'm freaking out because in that moment you made me feel things I've never felt with anyone before, and I realized how much I like you and that scares the shit out of me because of my fucked-up childhood.* Can't exactly say that, though, can I? Running isn't great either, but it was my only option, unless he'd enjoy seeing the tears I'm so desperately trying to hold back.

"Nothing, I'm just cleaning up."

"Did I hurt you?"

"No! I'm fine, just give me a minute."

"Okay," he says gently, and I hear one more tap on the door before the sounds of him moving away. I use the toilet and clean up because, for the first time ever, I didn't use a condom—my need to feel him was too great in the moment. Taking one last deep breath to push the emotions down, I grab a towel and walk back out.

Ezra sits on the edge of the bed with his trousers back on, and he holds a hand out for me. I take it easily, and he pulls me down so I'm straddling him.

"Did I hurt you?" he asks gently, tracing my shoulder, and when I look there's slight teeth-marks from where he bit me when he came.

"Not at all," I say truthfully. Actually, I kind of like his mark on me.

"Are we good?" he asks, searching my face.

"Yeah, of course."

"Do you want me to go?" He rests his head against me while I think. Do I? Fuck. I don't know. None of what I'm feeling is negative, but it scares the shit out of me, and I don't want to scare the shit out of him. When I don't answer, he cups my face and kisses me gently, taking my nonanswer as an answer itself. "I'm gonna go, but only to give you some space. If you want me to come back, just text me. I'll be here right away."

"Okay." I nod, and he drops a light kiss on my lips again. I listen for the door, and when he's gone, I let a few tears out. Just a few, for the poor girl inside me—the one not quite right enough to take a risk, who is so overwhelmed by genuine feelings she hasn't had years to get used to, so surprised by a decent man that it's too much. Then I get dressed in sweats and stare at my phone, wanting to text Ezra so badly it hurts, until a knock makes me jump and Sawyer pokes his head around the door.

"Hey, you still up?"

"Yeah." I smile at him, but his eyes tighten anyway. He can read me like a book.

"What's up?"

"Nothing." He silently raises a brow, calling me on my obvious lie, and I want to fall into our comforting relationship, where he's just my best friend who knows exactly how to make me feel better and nothing is awkward.

Finally, I cave. "I've got some emotional baggage, you know?"

"Ice cream fixes all of that," he says. "I'll meet you on the sofa." Then he's gone, and I do join him on the sofa, spending the night eating my feelings with my head resting on the shoulder of my best friend and pretending that it's all that simple.

Chapter 18

Ezra

I WORRY ABOUT HARLOW all night, hoping I didn't actually hurt her. I don't think I was overly rough, but she made me lose my mind a little bit. The bite mark proves that. Her body is insane—those perfect tits, and her tiny waist. Then the sounds she makes, showing exactly what she likes and what she loves. Shit, I'm getting hard again just remembering it. But she closed down at the end.

Maybe it wasn't good for her? Maybe she doesn't like to be marked. Maybe she's a spectacular actress, because watching her come was the sexiest thing I've ever seen. But maybe she faked it. Fuck, I don't know. I wish I hadn't left, but I felt like she was uncomfortable with me there, and that's the last thing I'd want, especially in her own home. I can't wait to know her better and figure out her boundaries—when I can push a little and when to back down. This second-guessing is torture.

I don't want to go back over until she texts me, so I get ready for work and leave without seeing her. I know she has work at ten, so she's probably already gone, and on the way in to work I finally hear from her.

Harlow: **Morning :)**

That's good, right? Seems pretty blasé to me, which means she's not pulling back. Maybe she's worried I'm less interested now we've had sex? I wish she'd just talk to me, but I understand we haven't known each other that long. I need to make it clear I'm in this for the long haul.

Ezra: **Morning. I hope you slept well. Are you okay? That's the last time I leave you alone when you're naked in your bed**

Harlow: **Deal. Redo tonight?**

A breath of relief escapes me, and my day looks up from there. The guys at the shop rib me for my good mood, but I don't care. I spend some time finalizing Harlow's design and take my tablet to show her how it'll look on her. Sawyer opens the door when I get to theirs.

"Hey man, how are you?"

"Not bad, and you?"

"Great. Where are you off to?" Before he can answer, Harlow comes out, pulling a hoodie over her head.

"I thought I heard you."

"Hey," I say around my grin as I meet her halfway, pulling her to me for a kiss.

"I'll see you later," Sawyer calls as he leaves.

"What's his rush?" Harlow's grin dims just a little, but she tries to cover it quickly.

"Eager to see Mandy, I guess."

"Who's Mandy?"

"One of his fuck buddies. Did you eat?" I can see she's trying to change the subject, so I go with it and call in an order to be delivered. When that's done and we're settled on the couch, I pull my tablet out.

"I've got something to show you."

"Oh yeah?" I bring up the program that shows her tattoo in place and hand it over. "Oh my god, Ezra, that's perfect!"

"You sure? I printed this out if you wanna make any changes." I show her the larger print of the full design that she could amend, but she gapes and strokes the lines with her fingertips.

"No way! It's exactly what I wanted."

"Not too big?" It's only her first, and I don't want to overwhelm the area if she's after something more subtle.

"No! How did you get that photo of me?"

"It's not a photo, it's an animation."

"You drew that?"

"Kind of. I wanted you to see it on *you* before you committed." I show her how it spins so she can see the different angles and check you can't see it from the front.

"That's incredible. The tattoo and the show-and-tell. When can we do it?" she asks, tearing her gaze from the designs for the first time and looking over at me with excitement.

"Whenever you want. Have you told Sawyer?"

"No, not yet. You're the only one that knows."

"But it's for him, right? The design, the placement. I'm pretty observant."

"Well, I'd say so. You drew me perfectly." She looks back down at the tablet, but I cup her cheek and pull her back to face me.

"Don't look so guilty. This isn't a berating, I'm just curious."

"About?"

"Why you aren't together." I know Sawyer has told me his side, but it's obvious to me that Harlow wants him.

"We aren't together because we're like brother and sister."

"I get that you're close, but I don't think your feelings are platonic. Before you automatically deny it, know that I'm not judging you, and I'm not going to tell Sawyer any of this, I just want to know everything about you. Including how you're feeling about other people."

"You make it sound easy."

"It is. I like you, and you like me, but you also like Sawyer."

She scoffs. "It's not as simple as that."

"Why not?"

"I'm gonna need a drink for this conversation." She sighs, and I follow her over to the counter where she makes us both a vodka and lemonade, downs hers, and makes another.

"We don't have to talk about it," I offer. "Obviously I want to, but making you uncomfortable is the last thing I want to do."

"No, it's fine. It's about time I found my balls." She takes her fresh drink back to the sofa, and I follow, pulling her over my lap so she's straddling me as she takes a deep breath.

"When I'm with Sawyer, I'm probably the happiest I ever am."

"Well, as fun as this is," I joke, and the corner of her mouth tips up as she rolls her eyes.

"It's not often I feel properly, giddily, freely happy. Sawyer makes me feel like that. And you make me feel like that." I don't move or respond, watching the myriad of emotions flick across her face as she bares her truth to me. "Growing up, I didn't have a stable upbringing. I bounced back and forth between children's homes and foster families. People were quick to want me because I looked like an angel, but I was just a scared, rejected kid, and I would act out. Nothing bad, not really. But when you're expecting an angel and then get a kid with behavioral issues, well . . . I guess any rebellion seems awful. I've never had anyone to rely on or have as a constant. Until Sawyer. And he wanted me to stay. Even as a child, he was vocal about wanting me to stay with him. He's the only one who has said it and meant it. He proves that every day, and he's there for me, no matter what shitty decisions or mistakes I make."

Her story tugs at my chest, and I want to wrap her up in my arms and promise her the world, but I know she needs to get this out.

"We had this pact when we were younger. It started as this silly thing when we were teenagers and hated the thought of having a girlfriend or a boyfriend. Everyone always made comments about us being together, and it made us uncomfortable at that age, so we agreed to only ever be friends. Then, even as we grew up and started actually liking the opposite sex, it just stuck . . . and now it's grown into something serious. I can't risk telling him, in case that's finally the mistake so stupid that he doesn't stick with me."

"Jesus, Harlow."

"What?"

"You know that decent people don't leave after one mistake? You're allowed to make them."

She shrugs. "Maybe in theory."

"Are you just waiting for Sawyer to be ready?" I don't think that's true, but I need to know before I throw myself into this relationship headfirst.

"I spend time with you because I want to. You kind of called to me, and I had to see where it was going. Now,

I don't want to not do this with you, but I also don't want Sawyer to have this with anyone else. Guess that's a problem, huh?"

"What is this?" I ask, gesturing between us.

She watches me for a second before her face drops, as if she's closing in on herself already, but her gaze sits right where my tattoo is under my top. Trailing her finger along the material as if she can see through it, she shifts nervously in my lap, and I clench my teeth as her perfect ass grinds on me. *Think unsexy thoughts*. As she looks up, her eyes sparkle, and she repeats the gesture. I grip her hips with my hands, keeping her still. "Harlow," I warn.

"I don't know. I've run out of words. Let me show you instead."

"Oh, you can definitely show me. But I need to hear you say what that means." I don't want any misunderstandings, and most of all, I'd hate for her to regret it when it's done.

"It means that this is going well between us, and I want to see where it goes." Good enough for me.

"And Sawyer?"

"Is currently with Mandy," she deadpans.

"That doesn't mean anything," I say.

"Doesn't it?"

"You said yourself, you saw men all the time."

"Do you want to hear something pathetic?" she says. "Just remember that I'm a strong, independent woman, but rejection is my weak spot, okay?" She's joking, but I can see the vulnerability in her eyes. "The only reason I pick guys up is so I don't have to sit and listen to Sawyer and whatever girl he brings back. None of them have ever even made me come."

"What?!" I can't believe it. Well, I can, but it's tragic.

"The casual flings. Not one of them made me orgasm. Yesterday, you were the first person who'd ever done that, and then I got so overwhelmed and fucked that up too. I stressed all day about you not wanting to bother with me now I'd screwed up and freaked out on you."

"Harlow! I wanted to stay, but I didn't know what was wrong and didn't want to pressure you."

"I think maybe I need a bit of pressure sometimes," she whispers.

"Deal. You'll be lucky if I ever let you sleep alone again." She looks up and smiles at that as I reach up to stroke her cheek.

"You don't think I'm fucked up?" she asks hesitantly.

"No. I think you're perfectly imperfect, but we all are. I don't want you to worry about that with me. And if you do, I want you to talk to me. Just like I think you should talk to Sawyer."

"I can't—" I put a finger against her lips.

"Not right now. Later. But just think about it, okay?"

"Okay. Why are you so determined?" she asks.

"Because I want you to be giddily happy at all times. I want you to have everything you want." She leans in close, until our lips are only a hairsbreadth away and I can feel her breath on my mouth.

"What if what I want is for you to kiss me already?" she whispers.

"I can do that." I grin as she closes the distance to meet my lips with hers. Grabbing her hips, I pull her down harder against my lap, and she gasps when we connect through our clothing. Focusing on a serious conversation with Harlow sitting right there was no easy feat. I grip her chin between my thumb and forefinger and drag her back to me, eliminating any remaining space between us with a forceful kiss. She wraps her arms around my neck, and I move my hand to her back, stroking up underneath her shirt and tracing her curves. She shivers in my hold, and I use the small break in our kiss to whisper against her lips. "Let's go back to the 'coming' thing."

"What about it?" she asks.

"I want to know what you like." I rub my thumb over her nipple and can feel the outline of what must be a lacy bra. "What are your fantasies? Sawyer can't be the only reason you saw those guys."

"No." She grinds on my lap a little as I gently pinch her nipple. "I like sex. Well, I like the idea of sex more than what I've had so far." Pushing her shirt and her bra cups up so I can reach her uncovered, I roll her buds between my fingers, pulling slightly as her back arches.

"What ideas?" She grinds and whimpers, leaning into my hands.

"Honestly, everything you did yesterday was pretty great." Ego boost right there. "And seeing your bite when I was getting changed today was *very* hot. I like seeing reminders of you." This gives me a couple of ideas to work with.

"Anything I do that you don't like, you tell me, okay? And anything you think you want to try, let me know."

"Deal," she gasps, as I pinch slightly harder as her hips pick up pace. I grab the nape of her neck and pull her in for another kiss. She pushes her hands between us and runs them down my shirt, but just as she reaches my waistband, the door knocks, and we both laugh as we lean our foreheads together.

"Rain check," I promise with a sigh. Fucking cockblocking takeaway.

Chapter 19

Nico

MY RARE DAY OFF is commandeered when I'm summoned home to meet with my father. It doesn't happen very often. Our rocky truce is stable enough for him to pretend he's happy with me studying and living alone, while I pretend the criminology degree I'm doing is to *help* the family business. Sure. I wonder if I'll make it to graduation before he calls me on my shit. Pulling up to the house, I square my shoulders and straighten my tie. Here we go.

My uncle greets me at the door, and I'm relieved to see him. He at least attempts to rein my father in, like the not-so-saintly angel on his shoulder.

"Hi, Uncle."

"Nico," he says warmly. "How are things?"

"Good, thanks. Any idea why I've been summoned?" He shrugs.

"Your guess is as good as mine. You know how he loves suspense."

"Is Clara around?" I ask, keen to stop in on my sister while I'm here.

"In her wing," he says. I'll see her after. I want to get this over and done with, and my father doesn't like to be kept waiting. My uncle leads me into Father's office, and there he sits. He's put on a bit of weight but is clearly not conceding that fact, seeing as he's still squeezing into the same suits.

"Nico," he says, devoid of any emotion.

I nod. "Father."

"Take a seat, son. How have you been? It's been so long since you were here." Ignoring the barb, I remain civil.

"Good, thanks."

"I'm good too, son, thanks for asking. Do you have any new information for us?" I pretend to think about it, even though I have no intention of giving him any information that would help his cause, not that I've bothered to gather any. Instead, I use the seconds to think about why I'm here. He's not called me here for idle small talk.

"I don't think so," I say. His jaw tics, but he doesn't call me out on it.

"Still enjoying your course, son?"

"Yes." I'm completely lost as to where this is leading. Unless he knows my intentions . . .

"Still working at that hippy café?"

"Yes."

"Is that where you met the beautiful blond?" Harlow. My insides turn to ice and I feel my eyes try to widen, but I'll be damned if I'm giving him a reaction. Creasing my brow slightly, I pretend to rack my brains, hoping it's enough to cover my surprise.

"Who?" I ask. He stares me down, but I've had practice, and I learned from the best. Him. *Never let them know your weaknesses*. If he taught me nothing else, at least he taught me that.

"I've heard about you hanging out with a gorgeous woman. Blond hair. Shapely. You know the type." I'm doing everything I can to control my body language, resisting the urge to clench my fists and ignoring my pounding heart.

"We hardly 'hang out.' She works with me at the coffee shop."

"And . . .?" The pregnant silence fills the room.

"And what?" I shrug. "She's a bimbo. Not really my type."

The words taste like ash in my mouth, but I'll say whatever it takes to take my father's interest off her. If he thinks he can use her against me, he will, in the worst possible way. His jaw clenches, and I know he's pissed he's not getting what he wants out of me.

"Well, I hope neither she nor anyone else is distracting you from that very important university degree." The course is a sore point, with Father having to bend a little and let me attend rather than keeping me locked up here to groom into a mini him.

"Of course not. I'm sure you would've heard by now if that was so." His lips twist into a smug smirk. I know for a fact he doesn't have people following me like Clara does, but I wouldn't put it past him to have a mole at the university at least reporting on my grades and attendance. Any reason to say I'm not taking it seriously so he can pull me out of there.

"Well then," he concludes with a wave of his hand, dismissing me quickly now he's not got what he wanted from this meeting.

"Pleasure as always, Father." I stand and leave the office as quickly as possible. My uncle follows me out to where I've parked my car, and it's not until we're far from the building that I let some frustration show. "How the fuck does he know about Harlow?" I ask.

"One of Clara's men mentioned it in their debrief. That a problem?"

I run my hand through my combed hair, messing it up now I'm not on show.

"No. I think he bought it."

"Bought it?" he asks with a frown. "Is there more going on?"

"No, there's not, and this is precisely why."

"You like her," he says. It's not a question, but I carry on anyway.

"It doesn't matter. Let me know if he doesn't drop it, yeah?"

"Of course, Nico." He pulls me into a rough hug. "It's good to see you, even if these are the circumstances."

"You too. Tell Clara I'll see her another time?"

"Will do."

I'm flustered as I leave, my cool definitely left behind in my father's office. I'm pretty sure I sold it, if his reaction is anything to go by. But that flash of fear of her being in danger solidifies my resolve to not get involved with her. It also makes me want to check if she's okay, right now, with my own eyes. Driving to the coffee shop, I speed just a tiny bit to get there before closing. I pull up outside, and Harlow's face lights up when she sees me through the window.

"Hey, what are you doing here?" she asks as I come through the door.

"Was just passing by," I lie through my teeth. I look around, and there's only one customer in here, but I can't see whoever is supposed to be here with Harlow. "Are you here on your own?" I ask.

"Yeah, Celeste had to run to get her kid."

"How long ago?" I ask.

"Like an hour? It's been dead," she says casually, but I feel anything but casual, and I try not to flinch at her ominous word choice.

"That's not the point. We work in twos for a reason."

"Alright, chill," she laughs. "We all do it." Yeah, we all do it, but not when it's Harlow left alone at night. "Good thing you turned up, then, I guess," she jokes. "Knight in shining armor. Or at least a pretty flash suit." She grins, definitely checks me out, and then blushes when she realizes I'm still watching her. She grabs a cloth and wipes the counter idly.

"I had a meeting with my mentor," I mutter, hating the easy lie and the fact that she thinks I'm valiantly protecting her when it's probably my own family she needs protecting from. Her face falls at my unenthusiastic reply, which makes me feel like an asshole. "Can I give you a lift home?" I ask.

"I'm going to the gym, but thanks anyway."

"My car drives there too," I tease, and a small smile lifts her lips. "Actually, can I join you?" Did I plan to go to the gym two minutes ago? No, but I have an aching to be where she is right now. After the insinuated threats from my father, I need to reassure myself she's okay.

"I don't really think you're dressed for the gym," she tells me with an arched brow. God, I really like this girl.

"I have spare stuff in my car, smartass."

I help her close up and we go over to the gym, meeting Sawyer for her hour-long PT session. He doesn't seem to mind me crashing, and I'm glad I did at the end, with the endorphins flowing and pent-up anger and frustration eased. Sawyer's staying behind for his late class, so I drive Harlow home.

"Are you officially coming over to the dark side, then?" she asks as we pull up outside her apartment.

"Definitely. Killer trainer and gorgeous workout partner? What's not to like?" My eyes widen as I realize what I said, but it doesn't seem to faze Harlow in the slightest. Instead, she frowns at the building across the road. "Harlow? You okay?" Following her gaze, I see the police car outside a little restaurant or takeaway.

"Yeah, thanks for the lift." She hops out but makes her way over to it rather than going into her apartment building, so I get out too and follow her. We step through what used to be a door and step over glass and wood splinters to reach the counter.

An elderly Chinese gentleman greets Harlow. "Hello, Miss Harlow."

"Chung! Are you okay? What happened here?"

He brushes her question off with a wave of his hand. "Just some teenagers causing trouble," he says. The damage looks like it was a lot more than that.

Two police officers make their way out from the back, their shoes crunching on glass. "Okay, sir, we've got all we need. We'll increase patrols in the area tonight. Anything else comes to light, we'll be in touch."

"Thank you, officers," he says. They nod as they walk past while Harlow still surveys the damage. It's absolutely trashed in here.

"Teenagers did this?" she asks again.

"Yeah," he confirms, but he's definitely lying, and I'd be surprised if Harlow hasn't picked up on it too.

"Do you want a hand tidying up?" she asks.

"I was going to board up the door and then leave it for tonight. My sons will help tomorrow. Thank you, though, miss."

"Let us help you do that." She doesn't ask it as a question, and we can both see she's not planning to leave without seeing this place locked up safely.

"Okay, but let him do the heavy lifting."

"I'd be happy to," I say. I get to work with plyboard that someone's brought around, and Harlow starts sweeping the debris into a pile despite Chung's protests. It doesn't take long, and as soon as it's done, he's ushering us out the back door—now the only way out with the front boarded up.

"You get home now," he tells Harlow. "It's not safe out here after dark." She gives his arm a comforting squeeze and starts walking down the alleyway.

"Teenagers?" I whisper to Chung before Harlow gets too far away.

"Keep her safe," he says. "They're hooligans."

"What really happened?" I ask.

"One of my sons pissed off the wrong gang," he whispered. It would be very unusual for the Seconds to target anyone who wasn't a Guard, but I'd have to check with the family to know for sure.

"Guards or Seconds?" I ask. My heart is in my throat while I wait for him to answer.

"Guards." I blow out a small breath of relief for my own conscience.

"Nico?" Harlow calls from the mouth of the alley.

"Coming." I nod to Chung and jog over to meet Harlow, having a quick look around for anyone in the area. It's after dark now, and the streets are deserted. Still, I wouldn't say I feel safe here.

"It was the Guards, right?" she asks quietly.

"Why do you think that?" She gives me a look, as if daring me to continue lying to her, and I sigh. "Why didn't you tell him you knew?" I ask.

"There's a reason he was lying," she says. "If it makes him feel better to think he's protecting me, then the least I can do is give him that."

Chapter 20

Harlow

I can't believe what happened at Chung's. I know it was the Guards, and the thought that they were so close—literally across the street from my home—puts me on edge. I wonder if they were there for a reason, or were they just this far out anyway? Knowing that would make a big difference, not that anything can really keep you safe these days. I should've asked Nico if he got any more details, but I didn't think to at the time.

Walking up the stairs to our floor, I spot Ezra on the phone just outside his door. Sneaking up behind him, I gently wrap my arms around his waist, and he covers my hand with his before pulling me round in front of him. Now that I know Ezra better, I can tell as soon as I look into Eli's eyes that I've grabbed the wrong twin. *Fuck.*

"Sorry—" I say, trying to step away, but he pulls me back by my hand and cages me against the wall.

"I'll call you back." He ends the call and pockets his phone.

"I thought you were Ezra," I say, trying to step to the side, but both sides are blocked by his arms, pinning me in. "Let me go, Eli." I push him in the chest, but he doesn't budge. What is going on?

"But *you* groped *me*," he says with a smirk, and I look up at him in disbelief. "What? Wrong one again? People are going to stop believing that soon. But don't worry, I can be the right one for you. I can be whatever you need."

"Doubtful," I spit furiously, but I'm furious at myself. He's right, I really do need to be more careful. How many times am I going to make that mistake? "I bet Liv would like to know that though." He laughs and I feel his hot breath on my face.

"Calm down, *sis*, I'm only joking." With that, he steps away and I make my escape, fumbling with my keys as I let myself into my flat while Eli watches the whole time.

What was that all about? Have I got on Eli's bad side or something? He's never acted like that before, and he's always been the doting boyfriend with Liv. But I'm not so big-headed as to think Ezra would choose me over his twin brother. Eli must know that too. He knows he can take advantage of my mistakes and I can't complain. And he's right. *I* groped *him*. And he was playing along as a joke, or that's what he wants me to believe. Even if we both know that's not what he's doing, it's a plausible explanation for everyone else.

My phone rings in my pocket, making me jump at the shrill sound in the quiet flat.

"Hello?" I say shakily.

"Hey, are you okay?" Fleur asks. "You sound spooked."

"Kind of. What's up?"

"What are you doing?" she asks. "Shall I come over?"

"Yes," I say decisively. "Bring wine."

It's not long before Fleur arrives, and an hour later, we're comfy on the sofa, her mouth hanging open as I finish the story from earlier.

"No way! What an absolute creep." She's outraged, and it validates my feelings on the matter.

"He is a creep, right? I'm not just imagining it?"

"No, of course you're not. Have you told Ezra?" she asks.

"I'm not telling Ezra." She goes to interrupt me, but I hold up my hand. I'm not telling him. "I started it. I groped his brother for the *second* time."

"Yeah, and as a decent human being, he should let you know he's not who you think he is and leave it at that."

"Isn't it my responsibility to check who I throw myself at first? And maybe he really was joking."

"Then he needs to work on his material. Why don't you let Ezra decide who he thinks is in the wrong?" Fleur suggests.

"Because what if he thinks it's me?" Her angry look eases, and I realize as my best friend, she probably understands the reason for my hesitation.

"You think he'll side with Eli," she says.

"Wouldn't he? He's his twin brother."

"Maybe he doesn't need to side with anyone. Maybe he can just tell him to knock it off." I shrug at the suggestion, not convinced.

"Whatever. I'm just going to stay away from Eli. Maybe I'll request Ezra only wears short sleeves so I can see his tattoos or something, and I won't be sneaking up on him any time soon."

I'm annoyed at myself for getting us into that position in the first place, but my internal berating is interrupted by Sawyer coming through the door, and I nearly drool. Maybe that's enough wine for tonight. But he's wearing a hoody and a backward cap with his typical workout shorts. It's my favorite outfit on him.

"Hey, ladies," he says as he sees us.

"Hi, Sawyer," we chorus, and he chuckles.

"I'm gonna jump in the shower."

Fleur is looking at me with one eyebrow raised by the time I drag my attention back from the bathroom door.

"What?"

"Oh, please. You're getting laid now, and you're still gawking at him. What's going on?"

"I'm not gawking," I say defensively.

"That was definitely gawking."

I shrug. "Well, he's hot."

"That he is, and you two get on so well!"

"Yep, as *best friends*," I agree before taking another sip of wine.

"I'm struggling to see how a boyfriend could be better than *him*." She gestures her head to the bathroom.

"I have a boyfriend. Well, something like a boyfriend."

"So you and Sawyer aren't happening?" she confirms.

"Nope."

"Okay, cool, 'cause I have a friend to set him up with."

"I swear I will hit you," I say. I glare daggers at her as she chuckles into her wine glass.

A minute later, Sawyer heads back into the kitchen area, and the girl-talk stops.

"Are you in tonight?" I ask. He's been out loads recently, and I miss him . . . in the way one friend misses another friend.

"Yep."

"Join us then, Sawyer! I need your professional male opinion," Fleur says.

"That sounds ominous."

Fleur walks him through her Lee situation, and he listens intently, but basically comes to the same conclusion that

Nico did—albeit a bit more tactfully. I let them chat around me and think about my own situation.

I know the reason I don't want to tell Ezra about Eli is because I really like him, and I don't want this to come between us. And yet, I know the reason I don't want Sawyer with anyone else is because I really like him too. This isn't some silly crush that'll go away when I'm not horny. I need to accept that this is something much bigger. I might have real feelings for my best friend. My best friend who has officially friend-zoned me.

And I know I should just leave it at that and move on, but I can't. I can't throw myself in with Ezra without knowing for sure what is there with Sawyer. Not because I'd choose one over the other, but because it's going to eat away at me, and I can't be saving a part of myself for Sawyer just in case he feels the same. It's not fair on Ezra. And I can't do anything about my feelings for Nico—I'm not a home wrecker—but I need to tell Sawyer the truth. Just to get some clarification. At the moment, my brain is conjuring scenarios which could be wildly misinterpreting the situation. Ezra's right. I need to talk to him and get everything out in the open.

Chapter 21

Sawyer

HARLOW IS SITTING ON the island when I get up in the morning, chewing on her lip and staring intently at her phone.

"Hey, you okay?" I ask.

"I'm good, how are you?" She looks me over, but I'm not sure what she's searching for.

"Why were you looking at that thing like it holds the world's secrets?"

"I was just about to text you, see if you'd be back in time for a training session before my shift?"

"Wow, you're not normally keen to exercise. Especially not this early. And what's going on? Why are you texting me? I was right in there." She shrugs, not seeming sure of herself, and I walk over and wrap her in a hug. "Angel. Is everything okay?"

"Yeah, I'm not the one MIA all the time," she grumbles into my chest.

"I'm just giving you some space," I say, holding her close.

"Why?"

"To be with Ezra." The reminder of her boyfriend has me pulling back and placing my hands on her knees. "How's it going?" I ask. I can't tell if I want it to be going well for her sake or going badly for mine. The reason I'm out all the time is because I can't bear to hear them together. Having random hookups is one thing, but this is totally different. And hearing Harlow come is a level of torture I'm not equipped to deal with.

"Fine," she says, "but you don't need to leave when we're together. You met him before I did."

"I know."

"Can I talk to you about that?" she asks.

"You can talk to me about anything, Angel."

"I guess I just feel like this could really be something." I get a twinge in my chest from those words, but I give her a small smile anyway as I step back to pour the coffee she's already made.

"That's good, right? Why do you sound so worried?" I ask.

"I'm not really used to it."

"Because you're used to people ditching you when it's not perfect." I see where all this is coming from now. "He's a good guy, Harlow. I wouldn't say that if I didn't think so.

You know I've always had your best interests at heart." I wouldn't. I'd never leave her with someone I didn't think would worship and protect her.

"I know, and I know he's great," she says hesitantly.

"I feel like we're talking about good things, but your voice suggests they're bad."

"Do you remember when we first met?" she asks. I blink at the change in subject as I hand over her coffee.

"Of course I do."

"Tell me," she says. She's asked me to tell her my perspective a hundred times over the years. I don't know why she likes hearing it, but I guess it reassures her that we're family.

"One day, I overheard my parents discussing the new kid that would be moving in with the family across the road. They had foster kids regularly, but they said 'This one's something special. She could be a child model. She's an *angel*.'" Obviously, I'd misunderstood at the time, but the idea of living across the road from a real angel fascinated me. "When you turned up and I saw you in the front garden, the sun behind you, lighting up your blond hair, I knew it was true. You had to be. Their kids always moved on eventually, but I knew I needed to keep you. My very own angel."

A small smile softens her face. "You've told me that before," she says.

"I know. Stalker, or what?" I joke, but her gaze is serious on me. "I marched right up and said, 'I need you to stay with me.' And you did."

"I did. I stayed for you." My brow creases as she gives me that information. "I tried not to make a single mistake, to never step out of line in that house in case they moved me again. Away from you—the boy who wanted me. Even at seven, I knew I wanted to be yours." Wow. I kind of just assumed she'd fit better with that family or grown out of causing trouble. I never knew she changed for me.

"And now?" I ask. Why is she telling me this?

"And now someone else makes me feel like you do, and it's weird. I guess I thought I'd always be yours." I'm stunned at what she's saying but can't work out what she means. Again, what she's saying is one thing, but how she's saying it is another. "Just because we've known each other so long, and you're like my safe space. I trust you with my life." *Fuck.* I think I felt my heart splinter in my chest. She feels guilty for needing Ezra instead of me. She's trying to say goodbye. It takes me a minute to formulate a reply, and she doesn't look at me while I do.

"Angel, I'm not who you should be worrying about." Those words taste like sawdust in my mouth, but the last thing I want is for her to not pursue happiness due to some unwavering loyalty to me.

"No?" she asks, looking up at me.

"No. Ezra is great for you. He brings out the best in you, and you're so happy."

"Yeah, I know, but—"

"Please, Harlow. Don't think about it for a minute more. I'm always here for you." The words are like a knife in my chest, but I have to say them. "Like an older brother, remember?"

Harlow's eyes are glassy, and she looks like she's blinking away tears. "Yeah. Yeah, of course. I appreciate it."

"Always, Angel. I've got to get ready for work." She nods, and I kiss the top of her head and turn, doing my best to not walk to my room too quickly, to not show how much saying those words hurt.

When I come back out to shower, Harlow has disappeared. I guess she's taken the chance to get out of her session now that we've talked. I hope she feels better; that she understands she doesn't owe me anything. I'll always be here for her, and I thank my lucky stars that I kept my word so far. I already know I can't come back here tonight and see her and Ezra all loved up on the couch. I meant what I said about Ezra being a good guy, but that doesn't mean I can sit there and watch a good guy loving on my girl. I just can't. Not yet.

Chapter 22

Harlow

MY GOD, I NEED a drink. I've never been one to self-medicate, but if I could erase the heartache, the embarrassment, the guilt from my system right now, I would. I should've kept it to myself. Not knowing was better than this. *Like an older brother, remember?*

He doesn't want me the way I want him. Have I fucked up our friendship by telling him I want him the same way I want Ezra? He let me down nicely, because this is Sawyer we're talking about and he doesn't have a bad bone in his body, but will he be different with me now? Why couldn't I respect those damn boundaries we've spent our whole lives erecting? I already had him as my best friend, why did I have to push him for more?

I can't even bring myself to tell Ezra I talked to Sawyer, even though he's the one person I want to comfort me right now. How can I be so happy and grateful for Ezra, and so heartbroken at the same time? God, this is such a mess. I need my other best friend and a drink.

"Are you going to tell me the reason for the impromptu night out?" Fleur asks before finishing her drink. Fleur and Lee were up for me third-wheeling, as usual, but I haven't been the best company. "I thought you'd be busy with Ezra," she says.

I shrug, but the mention of his name makes me feel guilty. I haven't told him about Sawyer, opting to come out and drink away my troubles instead, although all I really want right now is to be in his arms.

"I'll get another round," I say. I've nursed my one drink so far, but they've both finished theirs, so I head up for something to do. As I get to the bar and wait for my turn, someone steps up next to me.

"Hey," they say, and I turn to look at the guy next to me. He's not bad looking, just like any average guy that normally frequents this place. A week ago, I'd probably have taken him home. Shame I have absolutely no interest in him now.

"Hey," I say with a polite smile.

"Can I get you a drink?" he asks.

"No." A familiar voice comes from behind me, and the guy looks past me, nods, and turns away again. Then I'm spun to face Ezra, who looks damn near edible in a black button-up shirt and trousers. "What are you doing?" he asks.

"I *was* getting a free drink." I actually wasn't going to accept it, and I'm not sure why I'm antagonizing him.

"Other guys don't buy you drinks anymore," he says, threading his fingers into the hair at the nape of my neck. The possessive side of Ezra speaks to something inside of me. I can't help but push it a little.

"No?" I ask. His fingers tighten in my hair and he tugs lightly, making me let out a small gasp as my knees go weak.

"No. Now kiss me. Show every man here you're mine before I bend you over this bar and do it myself." Christ, that's hot. I push up on my tiptoes and give him a light peck on the lips, intending to pull away, but he uses his grip on me to hold me in place, devouring my mouth until my fists are in his shirt, my tongue batting with his, and I'm about ready to beg him to take me home. Then he pulls back.

"Enjoy your night, be safe, and stay the fuck away from other guys. I'll be over there when you're ready to go." He saunters over to where his friends are, and I try to ignore him and the ache he's started in me. Breathless, I turn back to the bar to order our drinks, but he's got my head all over the place. Why did I even come here? I could've been at home being kissed like that all along.

"I can feel the sexual tension between you across the room," Fleur says as I return. "Why are you still here?"

I shrug. "I'll go to him when I'm ready to leave."

"Go on, then," she says. "He's shown you and everyone here his cards." She's right. Going to him to leave isn't a test, it's Ezra giving me the freedom to enjoy my night while letting me know he's here for me when I'm ready. Why do I keep turning everything into a big deal? This is all terrifying to me, but I need to go with my gut instead of trying to prove I don't need him at every turn.

"You really don't mind if I bail early?" I ask.

"Not at all. Netflix and the sofa sounds pretty good to us right now." I hug them both goodbye and then make my way over to Ezra. He watches my every step with hungry eyes until I'm in front of him.

"You have a habit of making me shoot my shot," I tell him, and he grins as he stands in front of me.

"Only because you're fighting this. Let's go home." He leads, and I follow.

"Are you going to tell me what tonight was all about?" he asks me once we're back at mine and I'm making us both a drink.

"No," I say, handing over the glass. He nods, but doesn't reply, taking a gulp instead. "If you're angry, then why are you even here?" I ask. I can't help but needle him, to be defensive and self-sabotage, because I'm worrying I've made a mistake. He's going to leave, and Sawyer's going to leave, and I'll have no one. I can feel my self-control slipping through my fingers.

"I'm not going anywhere," he says defiantly, but without raising his voice. "I just don't like the idea of someone thinking they have a shot with my girl when they don't deserve it."

"How is it any different to you convincing me to pursue things with Sawyer?" I'm starting to yell. I know it's not fair to blame Ezra for what happened earlier, but my heart is bruised, and I'm a little buzzed and not thinking logically. "Why do you get to decide who I can see?" I ask.

"I don't," he says as he walks over to me. "*You* do. When your eyes warm when you see me. When your muscles relax when you notice I'm around. When you take that tiny inhale when I touch you—you do those things for them too. *You* decide, Harlow, always, so don't try to kid either of us that you wanted that guy earlier." My eyes are tearing, and I can't meet his gaze. "I don't know what you want from me," he says.

"I want you to want me." *Want me like Sawyer and Nico don't*, my heart begs. The words are barely out before his lips are crashing down on mine, and he speaks into my mouth between kisses.

"Fuck, Harlow. I do want you. You're mine." He cups me between my legs, and my stomach clenches with anticipation. "This is mine," he says, gripping me tightly under my skirt. "You and I both know who I'll share with. And when that happens, I'm gonna enjoy watching them take it." His hand is moving, and it feels so good my brain is scrambled. I moan as I try to decipher what he just said. "But if you need a reminder of who you belong to right now," he continues, "then that can be arranged. Get on your knees." He pulls back, leaving me swaying in surprise at the sudden loss of his body.

"What?"

"On your knees, Harlow. We're taking things up a notch," he says, his tone authoritative as he undoes his trousers.

I don't know why I do what he says. It might be the command. It might be because I want him to claim me. It might be because I love to know I can affect him like he affects me, or it might be because when I feel like I'm losing control, he takes the reins. But for whatever reason, as gracefully as I can, I slide down onto my knees. It's not until he's feeding himself into my mouth that I fully register where we are, and that I don't live alone. Ezra's gaze is focused on my face as I tense, and my eyes flick to the door.

"What?" he says, slowly pushing his tip over my tongue. "You don't want Sawyer to see you on your knees for me?" My face flushes even hotter. I don't know which I'm feeling more—embarrassed or aroused at the idea. "Hungry for my cock?" he growls. With a hard thrust, he pushes to the back of my throat. "Wet and on edge from being used?" he grits out, and I moan around his length as I look up at him. "Fuck, Harlow."

He pushes in a touch further, and my throat restricts as I gag. I can't take it anymore. Filled with so much tension and *need*, I'm desperate for release. I drop my hand down between my legs to try and release some of the tension coiling there. "Don't you dare," Ezra scolds, leaning down to push my arm away. I look up at him, begging, but his eyes are molten, and knowing I'm doing that to him makes my skin feel on fire.

"Good girl," he praises, cupping my stretched jaw and swiping his thumb along my lower lip, grazing where it meets his cock. My eyes water as he pumps in and out, and I let them drop closed for just a moment, but I push my own pleasure to the side and focus back on his face so I can watch him come undone.

I hollow my cheeks and suck as he pushes deep again, and he picks up the pace, groaning as he tangles his hand in the hair on the back of my head and fucks my mouth. And I fucking love it. One little touch of my clit, just the slightest pressure and I could explode. How does he have me so close just by using me? No one has ever played with my arousal like this before.

His breathing picks up as he looks down at me. I can feel how flushed I am, feel my watering eyes running over to leave tear streaks down my face and the slight burn around my lips where he stretches my mouth, using me for his pleasure. "God, that's a pretty picture, Harlow."

His pace falters, and he thrusts once, twice more, using the back of my head to hold himself in my throat as he spills straight down it and I gag around his release. As he pulls out, I gasp in a breath. I swallow and go to wipe around my mouth, but he pulls me up and sits me on the counter before pushing me to lay down. "God, that felt so good, Harlow. And you're so wet—I knew you'd love it a little rough. I can't wait to make you feel that way."

I don't get to comprehend what he's said, let alone answer, before he has his mouth on me. He swirls his determined tongue around my swollen clit and slides two fingers into my soaked passage, immediately giving me the release I crave as my vision goes white and pleasure blitzes my senses.

When I wake up the next morning, still naked and burrowed into Ezra's chest and surrounded by his scent, I feel so safe and content. My heart aches at the recognition that this feeling is usually reserved for Sawyer, and the constant happiness mixed with the sadness is frustrating. I still have Sawyer in the exact way I've always had him. I just have Ezra now, too.

I stretch back so I can press my lips to Ezra's neck and then his jaw, and he hums an appreciative sound. Trailing my hand down from his side to his pelvis, I stroke teasingly until his hips give a lazy pump, and then I take him in my palm, drawing a groan from his throat.

"Good morning," I murmur, my lips pressed against his neck.

"Mmmm. Morning," he replies as he pulls my leg up and over his hip, pulling me toward him. I line him up and he sinks into me slowly. A soft gasp leaves me as he fully enters me before leisurely thrusting his hips, building a slow-moving orgasm that runs all the way through me, from my toes up to my head. When we're both sated and our breathing has evened out, I realize Ezra's pulled me back into his arms, and I wonder if he's fallen back asleep.

"I told Sawyer," I say quietly into his chest, and he stiffens, shuffling to try to see my face.

"When?" he asks.

"Yesterday."

"And?"

"He doesn't feel the same." I bury my face into his pec, turning away so he doesn't have to see the lie across my face when it comes. "It's okay. We're best friends. That's enough for me."

He's quiet for a minute before he replies. "Okay." He kisses the top of my head and swats my ass, making me jump. "Well, seeing as we're awake early—best wake-up call ever, by the way—let's get up."

I groan. "Why?? It's so early!" He chuckles at my reticence.

"I can fit you in for your tattoo if we get up now."

My head pops straight up as I look at him. "Really?"

"Assuming you still want it?" he says.

"I do." We're still best friends, and whether Sawyer wants more or not, he's still the best person I know and the best thing that's ever happened to me. He's been my rock for the last thirteen years.

"Let's go, then."

We're the first ones there to open the shop for the day, and I sit on Ezra's bench and watch him while he methodically sets everything up. When he prints the transfer, I lay facedown on the chair so he can place the tattoo stencil before showing me in the mirror.

"It's beautiful," I grin, so excited it's actually happening.

"Good. Lay back down, then."

It only takes a couple of hours, and the shop is filling up by the time we're finished. Everyone shouts greetings to us and coos over what Ezra has done so far. I'm sore, but it's not too bad, and I nearly forget the pain completely when he shows me it finished, I'm that ecstatic with it.

"Keep this on for now, we'll take it off later," he says.

"Okay," I agree, turning to look at him as I beam. "Thank you so much! It's perfect."

He grins back at my obvious happiness, and I reach up to kiss him, showing my gratitude through actions, which is way easier for me. The other artists clap and wolf whistle at our PDA, and I blush, pulling away and ducking my head, but Ezra's not having that. He dips his head himself, chasing my lips and stealing another breathtaking kiss.

"I'm never gonna be embarrassed about kissing you, Harlow," he says against my lips, adding one last kiss before standing back and turning to tidy his space. I hang out for a little bit, enjoying the busy hum of Vice Ink, until my phone pings with a message from Fleur asking me to cover the café for the afternoon shift. After saying goodbye to everyone, I stop at home to change before heading over. I expect to relieve Fleur, but Brian is the one to run out the door when I get there.

"I thought I was covering you?" I ask her as she makes coffees.

"No, you're covering for Nico. I covered his lunch shift, but Brian can't stay for the afternoon."

"You've been here since six? Why didn't you call me?" I ask, hurriedly putting my apron on to dive into the late lunch rush.

"I don't mind," she says.

"Where's Nico?" I ask, but she shrugs.

"Just said he was sick," she says, placing down a coffee and turning her attention back to the queue. I don't think Nico has called in sick once since we've worked here, and straight away, I start to plan my coffee-and-cake delivery.

Chapter 23

Nico

I'M WALLOWING IN PAIN and self-pity when there's a knock at the door. It's unusual for me to have unexpected visitors, and I'm not expecting anyone today. Checking the peephole, I curse under my breath. I should've guessed.

I brace myself for her reaction and open the door. Harlow's smile drops, along with the coffee cup and bag she's holding, as she takes in my face. Ezra and Sawyer also gape from behind her, and it's completely silent, except for the quiet sound of coffee trickling down the wall beside my door.

"What the fuck, Nico?!" Harlow finally asks. Ezra bends to stand the cup upright, although it's futile—the coffee has already made a run for it.

"Hey," I say lamely. "What are you guys doing here?"

Harlow doesn't answer, just standing there with her mouth still slightly agape, so Sawyer does instead. "Harlow heard you were sick and wanted to bring you coffee and cake. We didn't want her to come over here alone."

"Good fucking job," Ezra adds. "What happened?"

I shrug, but then wince, and Harlow's eyes tighten with sadness.

I sigh. "They got me. Was bound to happen at some point. I swear it looks worse than it is."

"It looks pretty freaking bad," Harlow says.

"Well, we can't all be models, Harlow." It's meant to be a joke, but the half-smile pulling on my split lip ruins the mood. "Do you want to come in?"

I step back from the door, and they all come through as I grab a towel from the kitchen to mop the coffee up. Harlow snatches it from me with a glare for even trying, and Ezra helps her clean up the spill as I fall into a chair. Once done, the guys join me on the opposite sofa.

"You're in so much trouble," Ezra snickers, and I throw a middle finger up at him. Harlow joins us and hands me the cake bag.

"I think I managed to save this," she says as she sits back between the guys. "What happened, Nico?" This is the third time someone's asked me this, but I don't want to give Harlow all the gory details.

"I stayed for a lecturer's office hour and got caught up in the fray on my way back home. Left it too late, I guess."

"You walked?" she asks, exasperated.

"No, of course not—but there's no parking on the street around here unless you're collecting or dropping off. I was walking back from my car."

"But they were only out the other night," she says.

"They're getting worse," Ezra mumbles. They really are. The beatings are getting more frequent, even for them.

"But only here, they never seem to go anywhere else," she says.

"Except Harlow told me what happened at Chung's the other night," Sawyer adds.

"But that was for a reason, they weren't just there looking for trouble," I tell them. Harlow frowns, and I realize I let slip information that I'd held back from her.

"Why would they when they can get away with shit here?" Sawyer explains.

"It won't be long before they spread their wings," Ezra adds.

"Could they be out tonight?" Harlow asks, and I'm unsure, but I doubt Ezra would've let her come if they were.

"No," he answers confidently. "There's some big event at their top club tonight, they should all be there."

"You can't stay here," Harlow tells me.

"Of course I can. I live here. I'll be back to work tomorrow, and it'll all be back to normal." I try to make it out as not a big deal, but I don't think I'm convincing her.

"No way, Nico!"

"Yes way, Harlow!" She narrows her eyes, and I can see her mind working.

"How bad is the damage?" Sawyer asks.

"I'm not sure, honestly. I don't think it's too bad."

"Stand up," he directs, and he does the same. "Can you get this off?" he asks, gesturing toward my loose T-shirt. I manage to pull it over my head with my good arm and catch Ezra and Harlow whispering when I resurface.

"What are you two plotting?"

Harlow's eyes catch mine, and she answers too quickly. "Nothing."

Sawyer pokes and prods at my torso and arm while I hiss and take deep breaths when he says to. Harlow disappears, and I hear her come back as Sawyer finishes checking me over.

"I can't one-hundred-percent tell without X-rays, but I don't think anything's broken. I think you're just badly bruised on your ribs, shoulder, and face. They're going to look worse before they look better."

"Yeah." I'd guessed as much. "Thanks for that." Sawyer nods his acceptance and I go to sit back down, but Harlow claps her hands.

"Let's go, then."

"Thanks for coming—"

"You too," she interrupts.

"Harlow—"

"Nico." She says my name in the exact tone I just said hers, and I try not to smirk. "I mean, I have all of your school stuff here, so if you wanna go back to normal tomorrow then you should probably come with us." She smirks, and my mouth drops at her casual declaration of blackmail.

"You little—"

"You can hardly fight me for it, can you?" she says sweetly, but I can still see the upset in her eyes.

"Even fully healed, I'd like to see him try," Sawyer mutters to Ezra. He gestures for me to follow. "Come on, dude. I'm starving."

"I can drive," Ezra says as he grabs my keys from the counter. "Go grab some clothes. We've got to make a move before the Guards get out from their event." He holds his app up to me to show the coast is clear, and I'm torn. I don't want to stall them and make them run into the Guards, and also, I wouldn't hate being closer to Harlow for a bit, but it doesn't seem like a good idea. In the end, it's the silent pleading in her eyes that sways me.

"Fine. But only for one night," I say.

When we're settled back at their place and have eaten, I fidget on the sofa as my ribs remind me that I took a beating less than twenty-four hours ago. Sawyer notices, and after glancing to make sure Harlow isn't in earshot, asks quietly, "You taken anything for that yet?"

"Nah, it'll be fine," I say. He rolls his eyes at my martyrdom and leaves but comes back quickly holding out a small container of pills.

"They're good ones. I got them for gym injuries."

"Thanks, man," I say as I swallow two down.

"I'm gonna head to bed," he says to us as Ezra and Harlow re-enter the living room. "Night, all." He doesn't hug Harlow, which seems odd to me—they're always pretty tactile with each other.

"You can take my bed," Harlow offers. "I'll crash with Ezra."

"No way. I'm not turfing you out," I say. "I'll have the sofa."

"You need—"

"I'm fine, Harlow. I'll be here either way," I say as I lie down, feeling the pills taking effect already. I realize they really are the good ones as the room goes a bit wobbly. Ezra chuckles and mutters something about a stubborn-off, but things are fading too fast, and soon I feel like I'm asleep and dreaming.

A soft, warm weight lands on me, but I can't lift my heavy eyelids to check it out. My exhaustion and pain have blissfully ebbed away, leaving only peace. I really like this stuff. I dream of a perfect blond angel, with kind eyes and a beautiful smile. She's here for me. I hope this doesn't mean I'm dying. There's background noise, but I can only grasp certain bits. What does the angel want to say to me? *As long as she knows you're safe, you're exactly where you need to be,* the angel says. My mind floats. *She does,* I think loudly. *She's perfect. She's mine. I think I love her.* Then my mind drifts away, and there's nothing left but relief.

Chapter 24

Ezra

I'VE GOT A LATE-NIGHT tattoo booking tonight with a busy client, so I take advantage of the late start and arrange a gym session with Sawyer. We head back to shower and change, and then I meet him at his place because Sawyer's making lunch, and that guy can *cook*. Nico finally stirs just as he's plating up, and a minute later, his head pops up over the back of the sofa, hair sticking out in all directions.

"Hey, Sleeping Beauty," I call out.

"Geez, those pills really knocked me out," he says, rubbing his face as he sits up.

"Good though, aren't they?" Sawyer adds, and Nico nods, standing and rolling his shoulder. "How's it feeling?" he asks as Nico gently turns his torso.

"Not too bad."

"They got you good, huh?" I say. The black eye and split lip are looking angrier today.

"Yeah. Three of them jumped me, the fucking cowards." Sawyer puts two plates down on the bench and waves Nico over. He gingerly sits beside me. "They were wearing their colors, so I know it was them."

"Get any good hits in?" Sawyer asks.

"Nope. Didn't even see them coming until I went down."

"You didn't give us these details yesterday," I point out.

"And let Harlow think I can't handle myself? No thanks." He's only half joking, and I chuckle because I know the feeling.

"She has a way of making you want to impress her, doesn't she?" He nods at my assessment, then realizes she's still not joined us.

"Where is she, anyway?"

"At work," Sawyer says. Awareness dawns on his face.

"Shit, I'm supposed to be there!"

"It's okay, she covered for you."

Nico grumbles and pats his empty pockets. "What's the time? I'll go take over."

"Gone midday," I tell him.

"Shit," he repeats. "I swear I had an alarm set. Now I can't find my phone."

"Wouldn't be surprised if she turned it off, although you probably would have slept through it anyway with that stuff," Sawyer muses.

"She's determined to look after me, isn't she?"

"Yep. Even if you did spend five minutes going on about your girlfriend when she tucked you in for the night," I tell him. I know it's not really his fault, but I hated seeing the sad, hurt look on Harlow's face. Giving him a little shit won't hurt him. Sawyer looks surprised.

"Not cool, man," he says, turning back to the stove.

"What?" Nico asks, perplexed.

"I know you were probably high as a kite, but still. She acts super tough, but she has strong feelings under all those layers of protection, and I think we all know she has them for you. So even if you don't feel the same way, maybe simmer it down, yeah?"

"I don't know what you're talking about. I don't even have a girlfriend. I just let Harlow think that."

"You're a fucking asshole," I say to him. What a dick. He has no idea how much he's hurt her by doing that.

"Ezra, come on. I obviously have a good reason." He tries to placate me, but I'm not having it.

"No, you don't. Whatever it is, it's not good enough. Not worth her feeling like that."

"That's my decision to make," he says.

"Then man up and stay away from her." I look into his eyes, and I can see he agrees with me.

"What did I even say?" Nico asks.

"Something about her knowing you were safe and how perfect and yours she was." His eyes widen and his mouth opens slightly, but he quickly shuts it down.

"I don't remember," he says. He's lying. But why? "I'm gonna go relieve Harlow."

"No, wait," Sawyer interjects before Nico heads to the bathroom. "She won't let you. If anything, she'll stay there anyway and try to do everything for you so you don't work too hard. Just let her do this for you."

"I'm supposed to be helping *her*," Nico emphasizes.

"What, with studying?"

After a slight pause, he nods.

"You can still do that. She did bring your stuff with you, remember?" I certainly remember the hijacking, so I'm sure he does too. Sexy as hell when a woman takes control of the situation like that. "I'm heading out with Ezra, but Harlow would want you to make yourself at home."

"How about I cook before I go?" Nico offers.

"Good luck getting out of here today, but I'm not going to say no to dinner."

"If there's anything you need that they don't have, check my fridge," I say as I take a picture of him for our home security software. "Just walk toward my door to get in."

"What—" Nico starts, but I'm gone, adding his face to our security system on the way so that he can get in keyless if he does need anything. I also send him the app that'll let him scan for Guards. If he's determined to head home today, then the least I can do is reassure Harlow that he's doing it safely.

Chapter 25

Harlow

FLEUR DROPS ME HOME that evening, and ridiculously, I'm hoping that Nico is still there. It would be unusual for him to have stayed all day when no one else was in, but you never know.

I rush into the apartment and stop short when I see Sawyer standing against the counter.

"Oh, hey." I feel like we haven't seen each other alone since *the discussion*. He's definitely been avoiding me.

"You okay?" he asks with a slight frown.

"Yeah, I just wasn't expecting you to be here," I say.

"I do live here, remember." His tone is light, but his eyes seem kind of melancholy.

"Could've fooled me." He doesn't reply, so I skip over it too. "It smells amazing in here."

"That'll be Nico's doing," he says as he passes me a note from the side table.

Gone home, thank you for having me.

There aren't any out, I promise. I checked before I left.

I'll see you at work tomorrow—I have a feeling my alarm will go off this time.

x Nico

I roll my eyes at the note. He definitely needed at least one day off to heal, and I'm sure he can't guarantee when the Guards are and aren't on the streets. He's just trying to reassure me. There's also some heating instructions for whatever smells so delicious.

"Do you wanna shower? I'll heat this up," Sawyer offers, and I gladly accept. I feel like I've run around nonstop for the last eight hours, and I probably smell like it too. Showering, drying, and dressing in sweats and a T-shirt, I go back to the kitchen, where Sawyer is dishing up.

"It really does smell good," I say.

"He's made enough to feed an army."

We sit down and eat, but it's not our usual companionable silence. It hangs over our heads like a deadweight. He scoffs his food and is taking his plate to the sink before he speaks again.

"How was your day?" he asks. Is that it?

"Shitty, but over. It must've been national asshole day or something, because each customer seemed grumpier than the last." This is normally his cue to ask me if I want ice cream or a movie night, but he doesn't, and I hate this gulf between us. I'm about to ask how his was when he turns back to me and frowns.

"What's on your neck?" Shit, how did I forget about that? It must be the angle he's looking at me from now, and my wet hair making it more obvious. "Is that a bruise?" I don't know why I feel reluctant to show him now. I'm still happy I got it, but it seems like showing him will reveal a vulnerability that should be protected. Just goes to show how far we've drifted apart in such a short amount of time. I should've known that Sawyer would notice. He's always been observant, especially when it comes to me.

"Oh—"

"Are you letting guys rough you up again?" he interrupts before I can explain. The disgust in his voice and on his face instantly gets my guard up.

"That's none of your business. You don't even know what happened last time." I didn't tell him that I ended that hookup as soon as the guy had gone too far, but I don't owe him an explanation. If I'm into that, then he shouldn't be judging what I like in the bedroom anyway. It's not like he has any interest in that with me, so he doesn't get an opinion on what I consensually do with anyone else.

"Then what is it?" he asks. I can tell by the lift of his eyebrow that he thinks he's calling my bluff, but he's so far from the truth, and he doesn't even know it. I don't have the words to explain anymore, so I hold my hair up in a ponytail, move it away from my neck, and spin around on my seat to show him.

There's no immediate reaction from Sawyer. Only silence. For a moment, I think he's going to ignore it completely, but when I go to drop my hair and turn back around, one of his hands keeps mine up on my head while his other strokes the back of my neck. His fingers are soft against the slightly raised and slightly tender skin, and his touch sends goosebumps down my spine.

"Angel wings."

That's all he says, and I don't reply. There's no need to. He knows what the wings mean. He also knows the placement—he kisses me there all the time. Well, he used to. Now I realize those kisses didn't mean what I thought they meant. The wings start at the base of my neck and extend up my nape. You can't see them when my hair is down, and when it's up, they're mostly hidden by a ponytail. They're just for me. I don't move, because the feeling of his fingers skating along my skin is exquisite. His touch is almost reverent. "Does it hurt?" he whispers.

"Not really." I'm not sure why we're whispering, but it feels appropriate in the moment.

"When did you get it done?"

"Yesterday." His fingers twitch as they carry on gently tracing the lines.

"Ezra?" he asks.

"Yeah."

Seemingly done with the questions, we lapse back into silence. I feel the gentlest press of warmth to the back of my neck before, voice cracking, he says, "I don't know how to be around you anymore."

If the emotion in his voice wasn't already enough to break me, the silence as he walks away does. I hear his bedroom door close before I unfreeze and slump forward against the counter. This is all my fault. The distance between us; the turmoil inside Sawyer. All my fault, because I couldn't keep my stupid crush under wraps, I just had to tell him. At the same time, I know I had to get it out. It was eating me up inside. It's so much more than a crush.

I don't know if it's a feeling that's gradually grown into something more, or if it's only obvious now there's a gaping wound where Sawyer used to be, but I think I might be in love with my best friend . . . and he doesn't feel the same way. He's spent years making it clear he doesn't feel that way for me, but I still had to ruin everything by telling him. *What have I done?*

Ezra is my first thought of comfort, which doesn't scare me as much as it would've last week. Unfortunately, he's got another late-night session with one of his tattoo clients. Thankfully, Fleur is up for a last-minute night out, as she's trying to act a bit harder-to-get with Lee to see if that changes the way he acts.

We're only one drink in before a bachelorette party adopts us, and I'm actually having fun. Not having to think about finding someone to take home to stop myself from lusting over Sawyer is really freeing up some brain space for enjoyment, and what better than a rowdy hens party to immerse yourself in? Our small but raucous crowd is making more noise than the rest of the bar combined. Fleur and I are heading to the bar when one of the girls runs over and grabs Fleur's hand, saying, "Hey, let's go!"

We spin to face the bride-to-be, currently trying to pull us after her. "Come on, you two! Time to move on!"

"Where are we going?" Fleur asks, laughing at the bachelorette's excitement.

"The next bar. This is number four of five!" The others are making their way to the door now, and Fleur and I look at each other, trying to gauge whether we're feeling up for it or not. At the same time, hands snake around my waist from behind.

"If it's not my cute little neighbor."

I shudder at the voice and the warm breath on my ear, and without even turning around, I already know it's Eli. I pull away and face him with a gaze hopefully withering enough to get him to back off. This was definitely not instigated by me, and it was definitely not an accident.

"Oh, come on," he says, leaning in to pull me close again. "I'll keep quiet, and you can pretend I'm Ezra." My mouth drops open at his words, and I choose to believe he's drunk, not that that's an excuse. I have so many obscenities I want to shout at him, including but not limited to *keep your filthy hands off me*, but I settle for pushing him away again instead. Fleur looks apoplectic. Finally someone else has heard him and can attest to what a creep he is. The girl from before tugs our hands again.

"Come on, car's here!" That makes our decision easy, and we take the opportunity to leave with them. Decking Eli would only cause problems with Ezra and might get us banned from our favorite bar, so as satisfying as it would be, he's not worth it.

As soon as we pull up outside the next bar, it feels like it's got a different vibe to it, but I assume it's Eli that's thrown my mood off.

"Where are we?" Fleur asks as we walk in and are instantly surrounded by men. The bride-to-be whispers excitedly back at us with a giggle.

"It's where my fiancé and his friends hang out! Try and bag one of these guys. The Guards make good money, and they're so powerful. The danger is pretty hot too." Her voice is full of wonder, but my blood runs cold, sobering me instantly as I realize exactly where we are. Keeping my head down, I pull Fleur behind me until we reach a bathroom. It's ridiculously fancy in here. Huge, with black gloss tiles and oversized lighted mirrors, and an actual seating area.

"Do you think we're right in their place?" she asks as soon as we're inside.

"I know where we are, and it's not good," I say. *We have to find a way out of here, now.* "This just got very un-fun. Shall we go?"

"I'm done if you are," Fleur says. I bring up the app on my phone to call for a car, but there aren't any available. Whether that's because it's a busy night or because they don't want to pick up drunks from around here, I'm not sure, but I wouldn't blame them for not wanting to come to this area, and this bar in particular.

"Nothing available. Let me call Sawyer." However weird things were left, he's always been there in an emergency. His phone rings out, which is odd because it's never on silent. I call again, just to be sure he didn't miss it, but nothing. I call Ezra next, and he answers quickly, but I can tell he's on speaker as soon as he picks up.

"Hey, are you still tattooing?" I ask.

"Yep. Another hour or so, at least. He's sitting like a champ. Everything okay?" I know he'd drop it and come to get us, but it's not his problem to solve. I can get us out of this. I'm not just some helpless maiden.

"Yeah, we're about to leave. Just checking."

"Oh, sorry. Are you okay getting back?" he asks.

"Yeah, of course! I'll speak to you tomorrow." He says bye and I hang up, looking at Fleur with a grimace. "I know you don't want to call Lee, but—"

My sentence is interrupted by my phone ringing, and I sigh in relief, assuming it's Sawyer, but my eyes widen when I see Nico's name on my screen. "Hello?"

"Hey," he says easily in the sexy drawl he has, and I get the urge to curl up and listen to him speak. *Put a pin in it, libido. Now is not the time!*

"Hi," I reply as someone comes into the bathroom, filling the room with louder music as the door swings open and closed again.

"Oh, are you out?" he asks.

I sigh as I remember where we are. "Yeah. We've kind of gotten ourselves into a bit of a bind."

"Everything okay?" he asks.

"Just trying to get home. Unsuccessfully, so far."

"Where are you?" I look around and read the name from the top of the fancy mirrors.

"Harlow, that's a Guards bar!"

"We figured that out, thanks. We're trying to get out of here."

"How are you getting home?" he asks.

"I've put in a request on the app but there's no cars in the area. I guess we'll just wait for one to become free." I hear shuffling and jingling in the background.

"No, I'll come and get you. I'll call you when I'm a minute away and pull up opposite the front entrance for you to get in." Relief and guilt fill me. We can get out of here—and soon—but once again, Nico is doing me a huge favor for no return, and he didn't seem massively happy about it the last time.

"Are you sure?" I ask.

"Five minutes," he replies curtly before he hangs up. Guess he's sure.

"Nico's coming," I tell Fleur, but she probably got the gist from my side of the conversation anyway. We settle in the seating area to wait.

"Oh yeah, he must live around here. What was he calling for?"

"I have no idea." I'm just thankful he was.

We wait quietly and nervously in the bathroom for Nico's call. The Guards have never started anything with women—that we know of—but I feel so antsy being surrounded by them in an area I'm not familiar with. The last thing you want is to get on their radar, whatever gender you are. He calls less than five minutes later, and I grab Fleur's hand and lead her back to the entrance. Before we get there, she tugs my hand and pulls me to a stop. When I turn, she's looking through the crowd of people behind us.

"What is it?" I ask.

"I could have sworn I just saw Lee," she said, standing on tiptoe and trying to see through the throng of people. "It must be a mistake," she says. "I'm sure he wouldn't be caught dead hanging out with the Guards."

I pull her the rest of the way outside and exhale a huge sigh of relief when we pull away from the curb.

"What the hell are you doing here?" Nico asks.

"We got swept up in a hens party," I tell him, flashing Fleur a look in the rearview mirror to not tell him more than he needs to know. I don't want to tell anyone about Eli just yet, not until I know what I'm going to do about him.

"That's so irresponsible, and on your own, too. Do you have any idea what could have happened in there?"

"Alright, Nico, we know. We didn't mean to wind up there. It was a mistake. Thank you for coming to get us." He doesn't say anything else, but I can tell he's seething.

We drop Fleur off, and he's still tense when we pull up outside my place. His jaw is doing this ticky thing, which would be weirdly sexy in a more appropriate situation. It's like he's having trouble holding himself back, and it's a side of Nico I've never seen before. Seeing as I'm pretty sure he's angry at me, I really shouldn't be finding it this attractive.

"Sorry you had to come out this la—"

He scoffs, cutting off my apology.

"As if that's why I'm angry, Harlow."

"Why are you—"

"You should get some sleep." His hands have a white-knuckled grip on the steering wheel, and he hasn't looked at me this whole time. I get out without saying anything else, but I turn back and see Nico watching me walk in.

I'm feeling oddly vulnerable, a little rattled, and more than ready for bed when I open our apartment door to see Sawyer playing tonsil hockey with someone on the couch. They don't even notice I've come in until I slam the door behind me, and they both jump.

"Hey, Angel," Sawyer says, but he doesn't take his eyes off the other girl as he says it. Apparently, he only has eyes for the woman currently glaring daggers in my direction. I'm planning to go straight to the bathroom but pause when I see his phone faceup on the coffee table. His eyes flit guiltily toward it, and I know. I know he ignored my call. But still, I need proof.

I call his number, and his ringtone rings loud in the otherwise quiet space, the screen lighting up as I walk closer. When I end the call, the number three is in brackets beside my name. Something so trivial, but it rips my chest apart. He ignored me. For this girl. Who's not me.

"Wait," Sawyer pleads as I continue to the bathroom, but I don't want him to explain. I know it's selfish to expect him to drop everything when I need him, but he always has. And now I've ruined everything by trying for something more than he's willing to give, something that he's always made clear he wasn't up for. I shower, wash my face, and try to hold it together as I wrap a towel around myself and cross the living space to my bedroom. Sawyer is on his feet as soon as the bathroom door opens, his friend seemingly excused.

"Harlow." The anguish in his voice makes me feel even worse. He shouldn't feel bad for this situation. It's all my fault. I deserve this.

"Can we not, Sawyer? It's fine, really. Everything's okay. I'm super tired."

I don't wait for a response, instead seeking refuge in my room and locking the door behind me for the first time since we moved in together. After getting into bed, I curl up and cry for my stupid heart that has a space made just for Sawyer—a space that'll never be filled. And the fact that it could've been—it was—filled in another way, but I fucked it all up by telling him how I really felt. I knew I shouldn't. I knew it the whole time, but I kept making mistakes until I finally made the one big enough for him to push me aside. I guess he hasn't thrown me away yet, but he's chosen someone else, and that hurts so much that he might as well have. I can feel the physical separation like a living thing between us. *I've lost him already.*

Chapter 26

Nico

HARLOW IS QUIET DURING our shift together, and I feel like an asshole for being so blunt with her yesterday, but *god*. Knowing she was there unprotected, so close to the Guards and everything that goes with them, infuriates me. The fact that I couldn't be there with her to protect her, that I couldn't storm in there to get her, infuriates me even more.

As we go about our usual opening routines, she seems to avoid me as best she can in the small coffee shop. I don't know if it's just me, or if she seems sad in general. Maybe that's wishful thinking—hoping it's something other than my actions yesterday that made her feel this way.

"How are you feeling?" I ask her when we quieten down.

"I'm fine, why?" she asks.

"Just wondered if you might be hungover."

"Oh. No, I'm fine. I didn't drink that much. Thank you again for last night, and sorry we bothered you."

"No worries, Harlow, and I mean it. If you need a lift again, call me. Okay? I'd rather know you got home safe than think you'd put yourself in a dangerous situation because you don't want to ask for help." She doesn't look convinced, and I don't blame her. "Really. I wasn't annoyed at coming to get you, I was annoyed that you weren't safe. Please, call me."

"Okay," she says. The bell on the counter rings, but before I turn to leave, she stops me. "Nico . . . why did you call yesterday? You called me, and I never found out why."

What do I say to that? Because I missed you? Because I had an urge to hear your voice so strong I couldn't stop myself? Thankfully, the bell rings again, saving me from having to answer.

"I should get that."

Once again, I'm summoned to dinner with my father, and an uneasy feeling settles in my gut. Why has he called me back home so quickly? I can normally go weeks without having to be back here. At least my ribs have healed enough that I can move without flinching. If he finds out that the Guards beat the shit out of his own son, he'll rain down hell on them, even if they had no idea who they were beating on.

"Where's the shiner from?" he asks as soon as I'm seated.

"Someone caught me in the gym."

"Oh, really?"

"Yes."

"Not someone in the running for Harlow, then?" Every muscle tightens with the reflex to defend, but I shut it down. The last thing I want is to have my father aware of how I feel about Harlow. And we haven't even been served dinner yet. This night is going to drag.

"Why would it be about Harlow?" I ask.

"It's okay, son. A father likes to know who his boy's got eyes on."

Shit. Somehow, he knows. I know he's not just fishing this time. He's too confident, and I was convinced I'd covered it well enough last time.

"Although I don't blame you," he adds, before letting out a low whistle. "She is gorgeous. That tight body. Bet she fucks like a porn star."

My feigned nonchalance is out the window when I leap up and pin him to the back of his chair with a forearm against his throat.

"Keep her fucking name out of your mouth," I growl. His eyes flash with fear, but that quickly morphs into excitement, and he chuckles.

"Okay, okay." I let him go but don't sit back down. "So there is a fighter in there after all, eh? Didn't know what it would take to bring that fire out, but clearly, we've found her."

"What does that mean?" I ask through gritted teeth, but he doesn't answer, continuing as if I haven't spoken.

"That's all I want from you, son. Some *passion*. Some fight to do what's right. I want to protect us from the Guards, and I want my family by my side when I do it." We both know that's bullshit, but I don't question him again, content to let him tell me what he wants while I rein my temper in.

I berate myself as I take my seat again. I *knew* he was trying to goad me, but it's like my logical brain and my body's reflexes were two separate things. "Sometimes protecting someone means doing things that we wouldn't want our loved ones to do," he continues. "Doing the hard things so they don't have to. It's maintaining order and making sure there's nothing more powerful than us that could hurt them. The only way to maintain peace is by having the means to enforce it."

I don't know what crap he's sprouting, but I want none of it. "If this is some bullshit scheme to get me to enter The Games, you're wasting your theatrics. It's always been the plan."

"Yes, it has, but it hasn't seemed important to you so far."

"I've been—"

"Studying, yes, I know. But there's nothing in that course that will help you, and you know it. Any information you have on The Games is from inside the family. You think we all don't want to be living it up in some bachelor pad, doing what the fuck we want when we want?"

Actually, no, I don't think that. I think he doesn't see the need for education or any space from the bitter, violent world he's created. I think he loves the power, the fear, and the chaos he creates on a whim. I also think he hates not having control over me, and this is what it's all about. I don't need his money, and I don't need him. The car is the only thing I've ever accepted from him.

"You want me to quit," I say, hazarding a guess at where this is all going.

"I think if you were insistent on protecting those you love, you wouldn't be wasting your time leaving them so unprotected while you attend your little school."

"You leave her alone," I say. I'm trying not to spit the words through gritted teeth, but I'm not sure I'm successful. I hate that he knows about her, and now he also knows she'll be my weakness.

"Oh, are we negotiating?" He acts as though there's not threats hidden in his every word, but I know better. The mere fact that he knows Harlow's name means there's potentially a target on her back.

"If you man up and admit what this conversation is actually about, then we might talk. You need me more than I need you, and I think you forget that."

"But now Harlow needs you too," he says. I scoff. I don't think Harlow has ever needed anyone in her life.

"And she's the only reason I'm even entertaining this conversation," I say. "It's the only leverage you have, so use this time wisely. If you go too far, that's it."

He grins a smug grin, like the cat that got the cream. "Fine, son. I'll leave her alone."

"You all will. She's off limits. And if you want me to cooperate and go along with the plans of the *family*, then you'll stand by your word."

He sucks in a deep breath through his teeth. "That's a big order from someone who happily lives on the outskirts of this family."

"What do you want?" I ask. "You want me to quit university?"

"You're stretched too thin, son. Worn out. Neglecting your obligations to this family. I want you to quit one—school or work. From now on, you'll be having a more active role within the family. We won't be cast aside until you deign to visit us when you have nothing else on."

"What does that mean?" I ask.

"It means you use this time to start preparing for The Games. It'll be you leading my team. You need to start training them, preparing them, and yourself."

I scoff. "Not doing your own dirty work this time?" That was news to me, but partly explains why he's let himself go recently. I thought he'd be leading the team for The Games, with me there as tactical support.

"I'll be ready to go when the time comes, son, but it's your turn to step up. The next generation must be fit to lead."

"Fine," I say. "Are we done? I'm suddenly not hungry."

"We're done. I'm sure I don't need to go so far as to offer an incentive," he says.

"*Incentive.*" I sneer. "Do you mean bribery, or threat?"

"Such callous words, but take it how you will. Pull your weight, and we'll leave you alone."

"I hear you loud and clear, Father."

I storm out of the dining room as if Hades himself is on my tail. I don't even notice that my uncle has followed me out until I'm wrenching open the car door. His hand settles on the roof of the car as I throw myself into the driver's seat. There's anguish in his eyes, and I wonder if he knew what I was walking into. I doubt it, though—Father keeps his ambushes close to his chest, and my uncle has always been on my side. Mine and Clara's.

"She's really sorry," he says softly, worry in his tone. Clara told them? But I can't even muster any anger toward her. She's forced to live here. Locked away from the vicious men of the world, protected by more vicious men inside. Not that she's harmed, but she's suffocating, I know she is. If she used the information to buy her some freedom, or anything positive, then I have to give it to her guilt-free.

"It's fine. Make sure she knows I'm not upset, okay? Tell her I understand." He nods and closes the door. As I pull out and head toward home, my breath quickens. The enormity of what I've just agreed to sinks in, and it chills me to my bones.

Chapter 27

Ezra

I WIPE THE SWEAT off my forehead, push my hair out of my eyes, and groan. "How much longer does this torture go on for? You better be making dinner."

"You're such a whiner," Sawyer jests. We're at the gym, and I swear he's a sadist. But sadists make for good personal trainers, I guess. I'd be madder if he wasn't doing all this shit with me . . . and making it look easy. *Bastard.*

"Is that a yes? We can meet Harlow on the way back," I say between breaths.

"Maybe," he says pensively.

"Maybe?"

"I'm not in her good books." He throws me a towel as he guzzles some water.

"Why not?" I ask. Just then, Nico enters, and I'm distracted. "Hey, thanks for picking Harlow up last night," I say.

"Yeah, where the fuck were you two?" he seethes, throwing his arms out and walking over to us.

"What the hell, man? What's your problem?"

He points a finger in my direction. "When *your* girl is trapped with the Guards, I thought you'd want to help her out." *The Guards?* What the fuck?

"What? She didn't tell me that. I spoke to her and she was fine."

"And what's your excuse?" he throws at Sawyer. To his credit, Sawyer looks gutted.

"I didn't answer because I was with a girl . . . trying to forget about her." He runs his hand through his hair and pulls at the end. "Fuck. I'm a dick. I harp on about being there for her, and as soon as she gets a boyfriend, I abandon her. *Fuck.*" As he paces the room, it's clear he's beating himself up over this, and I completely understand why.

"Fuck, man. That's messed up."

"What is your issue?" Nico asks him, although we could ask Nico the same thing.

"Sawyer thinks Harlow needs him as a big brother, a constant in her life that doesn't want to get into her pants," I explain.

"Can't you be her brother *and* her boyfriend?"

"That's a really fucking creepy way to put it," Sawyer says, "but she doesn't want me like that. I'm glad I didn't ruin what we do have by being just another guy who wants her body over what she needs, but pulling away because she wants someone else is a dick move. I need to get my shit together."

"What are you talking about?" I ask, not able to make any sense of what he's just said.

"I fucked up. God, I fucked up, but I tried, okay? I tried for *years*, but I can't seem to hide it anymore. It seeps out in the way I touch her, the way I look at her. I'm not trying to make her uncomfortable, but I know I am. I've seen it." He sounds so defeated that I can't hold it back any longer.

"Then what is your problem? She told me she told you how she felt." Maybe we shouldn't be talking about this without her, but I think it's time all this came out into the open.

"Yeah, she told me she was pursuing things with you so I had to be put to the side. And I agree—she needs to see if you can make her happy—and fucking hell, Ezra, you'd better make her happy, because if you don't . . ."

"What did she say?" Nico asks before I can answer.

Sawyer runs a hand over his face. "She said she'd met someone else who makes her feel like I do, and it was weird, because she always thought she'd be mine." There's silence as Nico and I both look at Sawyer, waiting for the penny to drop. "What?" he asks when neither of us react any further.

"Nico, you're up, I can't." I turn away, taking the time to wipe down the machine as I try to wrap my head around this. No wonder she's seemed out of sorts. I can't believe he took that the way he did. Clearly these two have some massive communication issues.

"So Harlow told you she realized she always wanted *you* to be who she ended up with," Nico spells out for Sawyer.

"No, she said guilt had her thinking she owed me loyalty when she wanted to be with Ezra," Sawyer says, but his tone sounds less confident. "Didn't she?" We stare at him as if he's just grown another head. "Fuck," he breathes when he's had some time to process. "I told her to choose you," he says, gesturing to me.

"Not that I'm complaining, but I don't think she got the best impression from that," I deadpan.

"Shit. *Shit, shit, shit.* I need to see her."

"You know where she is, asshole," I say as he grabs his phone and his keys. "Just know I'm still her favorite."

Sawyer huffs a laugh as he runs out the door, off to declare his feelings to my girl. Is it kind of weird that I'm excited for her? No matter what happens, I want her to be happy, and if Sawyer's what it takes for her to be happy, then so be it.

I turn back to Nico, who is staring confusedly between the door and my grin. I raise a brow at his obvious questions, but he raises his hands instead. "None of my business," he says, shaking his head.

"Sure." *Yet*, I think. By the time I next see my girl, she'll have gotten over this whole miscommunication with Sawyer. Maybe I should be worried—they've known each other for most of their lives, after all—but I'm pretty secure in our relationship. Harlow and I are endgame. Whether it'll be *just* us or not, now that's another question.

Chapter 28

Sawyer

As I jog to the coffee shop, I run through everything Harlow said, and everything I said in return. I can't believe how dense I was. I was so worried about making her uncomfortable and being there for her that I didn't even think she could have meant something other than what I was hearing.

Stopping outside the coffee shop door, I see her through the glass, smiling at the customers as she hands them their drinks. My god, she's stunning. Even seeing her every day doesn't dull that to me. Harlow is the most beautiful woman I've ever seen. And she has romantic feelings for me?

This is it. This is the moment. Am I really going to risk our whole friendship for the chance to kiss her? What if Ezra got it wrong? I know now in my gut that I've been blind this whole time. I'm also really fucking terrified. This is *Harlow*. What if I'm not good enough for her? But I can be. I will be.

For Harlow, I would do anything. It'll be worth it to call her mine.

Pushing inside, I walk up to the counter, smiling at Celeste as I ignore the register and stand behind the last guy waiting for his drink. She sees me as she turns, hands him his drink, and I step up as he leaves.

"Hey, what are you having?" she asks with a smile, but I'm not here for a drink.

"What did you mean," I ask, "when you said you always thought you'd be mine?" She opens her mouth, but nothing comes out. Her eyes flick around, seeing who can hear us.

"I've got this if you need a minute," Celeste whispers. There's no one waiting to be served anyway.

"Thanks, Celeste," Harlow says with an appreciative smile as she lifts the counter and I follow her through to the back.

"What did you mean?" I ask again when we're alone.

"It sounds like you know."

"Maybe I need you to spell it out for me." She doesn't though, and honestly, I don't blame her. She's already tried once, and I effectively shut it down in my misguided attempt to read her mind and do what was best for her. Her eyes are full of vulnerability as she waits me out, and it makes my decision for me. "Okay. I'm not going to gently tip us over this edge, it's gonna take a shove."

I step closer and cup her jaw softly in my hand. Still, her eyes don't leave mine. "I love you, Harlow. I'm pretty sure

I've loved you since I was eight years old, from the first time I saw you in that garden, and there's not been one day since where I haven't felt it. I love you as a person, as a friend, but fuck—I'm *in love* with you, Angel. I would've tried to hide it forever if I thought it was best for you, but I don't think it is now." She still hasn't replied, and her mouth parts as her eyes flick through a myriad of emotions. "Is it?" I ask. It feels like an eternity before she replies, but in the end, she says all I need to hear.

"No."

I crash my mouth down to hers as if the chance will be taken from me if I'm not quick enough. I don't care that I've just poured my heart out and she gave me one syllable, that one syllable has made my year. I cradle her face in my hands and I kiss her with everything I have, everything I've felt for all this time, and it feels like coming home. Something expands in my chest that is all Harlow. I'm high on her taste, and as she clings to my wrists and kisses me right back, I kiss her until I forget where we are. Eventually, I break away for air, and we're both breathing heavily, her soft puffs of warm breath panted against my lips. Curving my hand around the back of her neck, I lightly stroke the skin that's still textured with the healing ink.

"I can't believe you got this for me. Even when—"

"You're still the best person I know," she says, interrupting me. "You always will be. Whether you want me or not."

"I want you. Fuck, I want you. I'm so sorry," I say forcefully, hoping she can see the conviction in my eyes, feel it in my touch.

"You don't need to apologize," she says.

"I wish I was brave sooner." I lean down to rest my forehead against hers.

"It's not about bravery. You were looking out for me, like you always are." She says it with such conviction, and I'm glad she knows intrinsically how much she means to me. I'll happily spend my life cementing that knowledge in her head. I stroke the raised skin again because it's always been my favorite place.

"You got a tattoo for me. I think I need to return the favor."

"I know a great tattoo artist," she smirks, and then her face breaks into the biggest grin I've ever seen on her. It's beautiful.

"Delayed reaction there," I laugh.

"Took me a minute," she agrees, pushing up onto her tiptoes to kiss me again, pressing her body into mine, and the feel of her is incredible. Indescribable. I've hugged her a million times and fallen asleep wrapped around her, but having Harlow kiss me, intentionally rub against me, is a whole new ballgame. I take a step forward and she steps back as I push her against the wall and our kiss turns ravenous. Unfortunately, the sound of the door chime brings me back to my senses. She is still at work.

"I should go," I say against her lips, right before I take them again.

"Mhmm," she murmurs into my mouth, making no effort to stop either. Finally, I pull myself away before I can't anymore.

"Okay, I'm going," I say decisively. "The first time I fuck you is *not* going to be in a coffee shop kitchen and with an audience. Not an audience of strangers, anyway," I add, and she lets out a small, shocked gasp and a laugh. I drop a quick chaste kiss to her lips before heading for the door. "I'll meet you out the front when your shift is finished."

"Do you wanna shower? I'll get us some food," I say as we walk into the apartment half an hour later.

"Or," she says slowly as she kicks her shoes and socks off before walking to the bathroom door, "we can order after. I think I might need a hand. I'm pretty dirty." Every bit of blood in my body seems to change course and head straight for my dick, and I run a hand over my face, praying for self-control.

"I wanted to do that properly."

"What does properly mean?" she asks as she slips her jacket off. I lean forward against the counter, clenching my hands around the edge, and her eyes dart to my arms.

"Candles. Romance. A bed." I didn't want to fuck against the nearest surface as soon as we were alone, but I'm definitely not against it.

"We've got time for all that," she says.

My dick pulses as she shimmies her jeans over her hips and down her legs.

"Worshipping you," I say, knuckles going even whiter as I hold on for dear life.

"Worship me wet," she counters, pulling her top over her head. She's left in nothing but black lacy underwear, showing soft skin that I'm desperate to touch. I push myself upright and let go of the counter.

"Multiple orgasms."

"Promises, promises," she teases as she reaches behind her, unclipping her bra and letting it slide down her arms as I walk over to her. God, she's perfect.

"You know what? Properly sounds overrated to me," I agree as I hook my thumbs into the waistband of her underwear, crouching to pull them down her legs. As I stand, I roam my eyes over her, absorbing every detail of her body.

"Me too," she agrees as I reach her eyes, and we both snap, reaching for each other as our lips meet.

I lift her with my hands underneath her thighs as she wraps her legs around my waist, clawing at my hair as we devour each other. Walking into the shower with her in my arms and my clothes very much still on, I flick the water on, turning so most of the cold blast hits my back before spinning to press her against the wall when it warms. Lifting her higher, she tightens her grip around me while I undo my trousers, line myself up with her center, and slide straight home. This is not the time for foreplay—we're both as desperate as each other to feel me inside her. As she said, we've got plenty of time for all that. I hold myself still, fully seated, and snake a hand between us to play with her clit.

"Sawyer, move," she cries as she clenches around me, and I struggle to keep ahold of myself. We may not be doing it properly, but I still have standards.

"Not until you come." If the tightening of her muscles inside and out is anything to go by, she's close.

"But you—"

"Do you know how long I've been fantasizing over this? I can't draw this out right now so I need you to come for me, Angel, so I can fuck you like the madman you make me feel like." I grit my teeth as I continue playing with her clit, and she does, pressing her lips to mine so I can swallow her scream as she writhes on my dick. Before she's fully relaxed, I tilt her hips using her ass and pull nearly all the way out, plunging back in to hit as deep as possible. She moans, arching her back to increase the depth, leaning against the wall with her shoulders so the only thing keeping her up is my hands and my cock. I've never seen a sexier sight in my life.

Keeping my pace fast and my thrusts hard, her fingernails dig crescents into my biceps as her orgasm returns, and this time, I join her, grunting as I bury myself deep inside her and we find our release together. I press my forehead to hers while we get our breath back, then slide out slowly as she winces.

"Sore?" I ask, concerned. Maybe I should've been gentler.

"In the best way," she says, and her sleepy, relaxed grin makes me believe her.

"Glad to hear it." I give her a light kiss before finally undressing and kicking my sodden clothes to the corner. She watches me the whole time from under the warm stream of water, resting her weight against the wall. "Enjoying the view?" I ask. Nodding, she pulls her bottom lip between her teeth, and I tug on her chin to free it before biting it lightly myself. "Behave."

Jesus. I could probably take her again already, but she's not just here for my pleasure. I want to make sure every time is enjoyable for her, which means knowing when she needs a break. I take a sponge from the shelf and wash her gently, and when she's recovered, she does the same to me. I stare down at her with an awe that I'm sure is written all over my face.

"What?" she asks.

"I didn't wake up this morning thinking this would be how it ended," I say with another kiss, because I can't stop kissing her. I never want to stop.

I step out, wrapping a towel around my waist, and hold one out for her that she steps into. Opening the bathroom door, she heads over to her room, and I point at the kitchen area before I go to mine, saying, "I'll meet you right here."

"Okay," she says with a smile. I go to my room to dress, feeling so happy I'm almost giddy. I'm just now realizing it could've been awkward moving from friends to lovers, but that was so natural I can't believe it's taken us so long. Drying and dressing in sweats and a T-shirt, I go back to the kitchen and find some leftovers in the fridge to put in the oven, setting the timer and grabbing plates as I go. Harlow joins me in a singlet and shorts with a frown on her face.

"Everything okay?" I ask, not liking the furrow in her brow, or the way she rubs her arms self-consciously.

"I don't know. I think I need to talk to Ezra," she whispers.

"About us?"

"Yeah. He wanted me to tell you how I felt—how I feel—but we haven't had an explicit conversation about what happens now. Neither have we," she says, pointing between us. She's tugging at her lip with her teeth, which is a sure sign she's stressing. Stressed is not how I want her to feel after the last half hour.

"Do you want to do that now?" I ask.

"You think he'll be okay with it?"

I smile, thinking about how he put me up to this. He knew exactly what was going to happen.

"Yeah. He was the one who made me realize I was an idiot. Him and Nico." She raises her eyebrows.

"Oh."

"Is that okay?" I ask.

"Yeah, of course," she says as she reaches over to grab her phone from where she left it on the way in. "And you're okay with it?"

"With you seeing Ezra too?" She nods. "I am. Didn't think if I ever got you I'd share you with anyone, but with him, it doesn't feel weird."

"You're sure?"

"I'm sure, Angel. Now check in with Ezra so you can chill out."

She types something, and a smile comes half a minute later before she puts her phone down and walks over, hugging my waist and resting her chin on my chest to look up at me. "Ezra said we only get alone time if you've earned it."

"Oh, really?" I ask. She nods. "And have I earned it?"

"Definitely." She grins. "Twice over." She giggles, and I can't help but return her smile as the timer goes off. We eat and chat like normal, and it's like the last couple of awkward days never happened. We're just Harlow and Sawyer, same as we have been for years. Except this time when she hands me her plate, I can kiss her instead of just thinking about it.

"That was amazing," I say, stretching in satisfaction.

"It really was," she says with a yawn.

"Early night?"

"Yeah, I've got an early start."

"Me too," I say. "The fundraiser starts in the morning."

"Oh, yeah," she says before yawning again. "Damn. I'm never this tired."

"Are we wearing you out?" I grin thinking of all the ways Ezra and I could keep her tired and sated. I may wind up enjoying this "sharing" thing.

"Maybe, but I'm sure I can find some energy from somewhere," she jokes.

"That sounds like a challenge," I say, pulling her in for a kiss. Her phone pings, but she ignores it, jumping into my arms again. I'm not complaining—if I could keep her here forever, I would. It goes off again as I walk her to my room, and I grab it as I pass, handing it to her as I lower her onto my bed. I flick the TV on and lay next to her. As much as a repeat sounds tempting, she is tired and sore, and I'm down for a good snuggle.

"What did Ezra say to you?" she asks, going back to our conversation from earlier. I'm glad she wasn't annoyed we'd been talking about her. I think for this thing between us all to work, it's going to take a lot of talking things out.

"He gave me shit for turning you down. I said I'd never do that—that it was the other way round."

She frowns. "I didn't turn you down."

"Well, I know that now." I hold her close, thinking of how miserable I was for the few days things weren't good between us.

"It was kind of scary, wasn't it?" she says pensively.

"Yeah, but only because we already have something so great at risk."

She idly traces my abs under my top, following the pattern with her eyes, and when I tense, she looks back at me. "I've wanted to touch you like this for so long," she breathes.

"The feeling's mutual." I roll so she's on her back and I'm leaning on my forearm next to her. I pull her strap down and expose a breast that hasn't had nearly enough attention. "Is it time to worship you now?" I ask.

"Don't let me stop you," she says as I trace the curve with a fingertip. Her phone dings again as I follow the path of my finger with my tongue. Cupping and massaging the weight, I close my mouth over her nipple, teasing the bud. Her phone goes again.

"Check it," I say.

She goes quiet, and when I look up at her, she shows me the screen.

Ezra: **I'm trying really hard to give you space but my fingers still typed this without my permission**

Ezra: **They're not the only part of my body that can't stop thinking about you**

Ezra: **Knowing that you can't answer because Sawyer has you busy is torture**

The last one has me grinning. "Sawyer does have you busy. Show him."

"What?" she asks. I bite down lightly on her nipple and she arches her back, pressing the mound against my lips.

"Show him."

A minute later, she shows me her phone again, and I see the little thumbnail of the view down her body, her breast in my mouth, back arched for more, and I see his reply.

Ezra: **Low blow**

I shrug. Not my problem. I suck the sensitive underside of Harlow's breast into my mouth and she drops the phone, weaving her fingers into my hair. Not her problem either.

Chapter 29

Harlow

WE GET UP TOGETHER, and Sawyer walks me to work on his way to the gym like we've done a million times before. But now, it feels so new. Everything feels comforting but also exciting. Everything is the same, but also different. I can't explain it. I'm glad Ezra gave us the night, even if I do miss him already.

"I'll see you later," Sawyer says before kissing me lightly, his fingers around the nape of my neck and stroking the skin there as he's taken to doing. He doesn't say anything about love again—he hasn't since his coffee shop declaration—but I'm pretty sure that's to give me space. I know he does, I see it in his actions, and soon I'll be ready to say it to him too.

I watch him cross the road with a wave and then walk in to see Fleur gaping at me.

"Fucking finally," she squeals, throwing herself at me. "I need all of the details!"

It takes all morning to get through the story so far, with constant interruptions from the morning crowd of customers, and when I eventually finish, she sighs wistfully. "You are living a romance novel, girl."

"I don't think romance novels have the girl with two boyfriends," I say.

"Oh, the good ones have a lot more than that," she says with a smirk, but the happiness doesn't reach her eyes.

"You okay? You seem . . . down."

"I'm fine," she says with a fake smile, brushing me off with a wave of her hand. "I'm so happy for you!"

"I know that, but you seem off." Her shoulders deflate a little at my observation.

"Lee has a job offer," she says.

"Okay . . ."

"A great one." My brow creases. I'm clearly not understanding something.

"Is that not a good thing?" I clarify.

"Not when it's a thousand miles away." Her eyes water as she smiles sadly at me.

"Oh, shit. What are you going to do?"

"Nothing," she says with a shrug. "We haven't been together that long. It'd be stupid to uproot my life so soon."

"Are you sure?" I ask.

"Yep, I'm sure. Oh look, a distraction! Boyfriend number three is here."

I immediately look to the door with a grin, assuming I'll see Nico entering, and then whip my head back to Fleur with a glare as I realize it's Brian walking in. She snickers, and I can't help a small smile.

"You suck. I'm going to the gym fundraiser. Have a good afternoon," I say, giving her a reassuring pat on the arm on the way past. "See you in a bit, Brian."

I get to the gym, and the main room is packed. It's a twenty-four-hour triathlon. There are people cycling, running, and rowing to substitute for swimming, so it can all be here at the front instead of using the pool. The atmosphere is great and everyone seems pumped, although I can't see Sawyer.

"He's in the back." A guy I recognize waves me over as he checks his watch. "He should be finishing up a PT."

I smile at him and head to the back rooms. Most are empty—everyone at the front where the excitement is—but a few have a class or one-on-one in them. As I walk in through the open door of the next room, I freeze. Sawyer is on his front, held up by his forearms, hovering over a woman who has her hand very deliberately on his cock.

Like I've been electrocuted, I step back and kick the door accidentally, making it rattle. *Shit.* My heart feels like it's being shredded. He hasn't done anything wrong—we never had the exclusive chat, not that he gave us any time to—and I'm certainly not exclusive. What if he assumes this is how it's going to be now? An open relationship? But I don't think I can do that. I want to skin that woman in there alive. How hypocritical of me. He's accepted it for me, so surely I need to accept it for him. I do the cowardly thing and run, leaving to spend my break at home instead.

I relieve Fleur, and she leaves with a smile, but I frown after her anyway. This Lee thing is hitting her harder than she's admitting. I can see it around her eyes, and in the slump of her shoulders. She's not the same Fleur she used to be.

"You okay?" Brian asks when he sees me watching her.

"Yeah, just worried about Fleur. How are you?" I ask, turning to face him properly.

"I'm good, thanks. Happy to be getting more hours."

"Oh, that's good," I say, making polite conversation. "How have you got those?"

He shrugs. "Well, with Nico leaving, they asked me if I wanted more hours rather than having to hire someone new." *Sorry, what?* "I think they'll get a part-timer to fill the gap and cover holidays."

"Nico's leaving?" I can't believe it.

"Apparently so," he says casually, as if it's not a big deal. As if I'm not losing seeing him nearly every day, spending hours working alongside him. Why did he quit? Will I not get to see him anymore? I guess so. After all, he's not even mine to miss, right? And maybe it's a good thing. I can't even handle two guys right now. Sawyer and I are clearly on two very different wavelengths.

I try to work the afternoon shift without showing how much the news has affected me, and I'm glad that Brian and I aren't that close, because I have the feeling I'm doing a terrible job.

Chapter 30

Nico

Harlow: **Have you got time for a study sesh today?**

I've been staring at the text for way too long. I want to reply and say *of course, I'll always have time for you*. But that's not true, is it? I'm going to be caught up in Games prep now. I should've quit university. My father is right. Any useful information and the bits I've been teaching Harlow have come from the family, not my course. But I need to separate myself from her, keep away as much as possible. I can't be around her so much and carry on keeping my distance. And now I need to more than ever. I wonder if she knows I'm leaving yet.

I'm in an awful mood at work as I try not to obsess over her, and after barely resisting the urge to shove a rude customer's latte down their throat, Fleur quarantines me out the back where I can't bite anyone's head off. I'm restacking the dishwasher when the door goes.

"Hey."

Spinning round, I take in Harlow's face. I wasn't expecting to see her today, so she catches me off guard.

"Harlow," I say.

"You haven't replied to my text. You can say no, you know?" She fidgets nervously with her fingers. Even though I've just spent the last few hours convincing myself I should say no, now that she's here, I can't.

"No, it's fine, I've just been busy. After work?" Her eyes narrow suspiciously, but she doesn't call me out on my obvious lie.

"Okay. Do you want to come to mine?" she asks.

"Sounds good. Although I'm running out of stuff to teach you, so I'm not sure how many more study sessions we'll have." I see the hurt in her eyes before I've even finished my sentence. She knows I'm trying to limit the amount of time I spend with her. I just don't think she knows why. Nodding, she turns and leaves, and my heart wants to follow her out, wherever she goes.

"And that's it," I declare, sitting back from my laptop and stretching out my back. Finally, after a double session, we've been through all of the material Harlow requested. I've given her what she asked for at the very beginning.

"Wow," she sighs. "That's amazing. Thank you so much."

"We've gone through everything. Is there anything else you want to add on?" I ask.

"Why didn't you tell me you were quitting?" Not what I thought she was going to say.

"Uh . . ."

"I thought maybe we'd become friends? It was odd to have to hear it from Brian."

I try to think of a reasonable cover. "Brian is a work friend too. I guess he just found out first."

Her face falls at being lumped in with Brian, and I feel like an asshole. Before either of us can speak again, Ezra walks through the door.

"Hey," he says to us both before kissing Harlow lightly. "Sorry to interrupt. Did I leave my charger here?"

"We just finished," I tell him as I start to pack up my things. I can't bear to be around her when it's me who's hurting her right now. It's for her own good. *Suck it up, Nico.*

"I don't think so, but you can check my room," she says. He wanders into it and leaves us alone again, and I nearly cave.

"Harlow—"

"Would you have put it away?" Ezra calls, stopping me before I can apologize.

"Maybe," Harlow replies before focusing back on me.

"I should go," I say.

"Harlow . . . what is this?" Ezra asks, coming back to stand in the doorway holding up sheets of paper. They're indecipherable to me, but Harlow obviously recognizes them, because she freezes. "I think you need to start talking." An intense silence blankets us, and Sawyer comes home right then, walking into the stalemate.

"What's going on?" he asks, checking on Harlow first and then looking at us.

"We're just waiting for Harlow to start explaining why on earth I found comprehensive plans on the Guards and The Games in her chest of drawers," Ezra tells Sawyer before focusing back on Harlow. "Are you with them?"

"What? No, of course I'm not with the Guards."

"Then what is going on?" Ezra says.

Suddenly, it all clicks into place. "You're planning to enter," I say in shock. Ezra gapes at her, and she sucks her bottom lip between her teeth, looking between us.

"Let's all calm down," Sawyer says, moving to Harlow's side.

"Calm down? Harlow, why are you keeping this from us?" Ezra throws the papers down on the table.

"I've only known you for five minutes," she reminds Ezra.

"Nice." He scoffs.

"You've known me for two years," I remind her, but her eyes narrow.

"Some things you don't share with work friends," she says.

"Tell us about The Games," I say, not wanting it to descend into an argument if I can help it. I need to know how far she's going.

"What about them? You're right. I'm entering. We're entering," she corrects herself, looking to Sawyer.

"For who?" Ezra leans against the counter opposite me, and Sawyer stands near Harlow, arms braced against the couch as though ready to leap into action.

"For us," she says.

"People don't just enter The Games," Ezra reasons. It is unusual. The Guards and the Seconds are the biggest factions, and a few other high-powered and wealthy groups normally try when The Games come up. Seeing as there's four territories in our state, and one Games for each territory, there's not a huge amount of people fighting for the spot. Not to mention those *weeded out* in the preliminary rounds . . . You need to be rich, influential, or just plain brave to sign up and make it through to the actual Games. Ideally, all three. To conquer the different rounds and actually win as an independent is near impossible. Harlow is literally putting her life in danger. And for what?

"Maybe not, but they can," Harlow says defiantly.

"I know that, but they don't. The powerful groups with all the money and firepower always win them with their fucking armies. The Guards and the Seconds and—"

"Yeah, and look how that's working out for all of the ordinary people who have to live here," Harlow exclaims. "The Guards are getting worse and worse. Your area is the worst, Nico, followed closely by where we grew up, and the territories are shifting all the time. The gangs are *expanding* all the time. Look at what happened at Chung's! There's so many innocent people who didn't sign up for this turf war."

"And you're signing up voluntarily," Ezra says like a plea, like he's begging Harlow to change her mind.

"The Seconds might win this time," I reason.

"You think that's better?! They're just as savage. They're monsters. We saw the fallout of them losing last time." The memory of meeting Sawyer's father, of what my family did to him, hits me like a bullet through the chest. She's right. We are monsters.

"And what if you enter and the Guards find out you're running against them?" Ezra pleads. "Do you think they won't make you an easy target?"

She shrugs as if that isn't a big deal, but I've felt firsthand how brutal the current generation of Guards can be. "We'll deal with that when the time comes. We might get kicked out so early they don't even notice us."

"And if you don't?" Ezra asks.

"Look, you're not going to change my mind," she says, folding her arms defiantly.

"I'm not trying to." Her disbelieving look shows she's not buying Ezra's shit for a second. "Well, maybe I am, but the whole thing sounds insane to me. Rich people pick people to do their dirty work for them, and then they take control. The whole system is so corrupt it's insane, and I don't want you to become known to them in a bad way, or worse, to not come out of The Games alive."

"The system is crooked, but the people they train are only *people*, just like us. They go through the stages like anyone can."

"But they have dispensable numbers to replace those who are injured. Who do you have?" My voice is getting louder, but she's not listening to us. She can't possibly think this is a good idea.

"Nico—"

"No." I shut Sawyer down. "You're not thinking this through. You can't do this. It's a stupid idea, and it's going to get someone killed."

"Nico—"

"Who is even doing it with you?" I ask.

"I'm in." We all face Ezra, shock on our faces. "My girl is in, then I'm in. I won't let you do this alone, Harlow."

"No offense, but you might hold her back," Sawyer jokes, lightening the tension. "She's fucking epic. We've been preparing for this for years."

"And I'm just a tattoo artist?" Ezra asks wryly. "Harlow isn't the only one with hobbies. You?" he asks, turning to me, as if it's that simple.

"Nico is brilliant," Harlow adds, causing Ezra to frown.

"Hey, I didn't get that faith."

She laughs, blowing out a breath at the same time as the tension continues to ease.

"I'm glad you're smiling again," Sawyer says, leaning down to drop a kiss onto her lips. She doesn't pull away and doesn't look shocked at all. When did that happen?

"Are you two together now?" I ask before I even think.

"Kind of," Harlow answers. "It's . . . casual."

"Is it?" Sawyer asks, looking half surprised and half pissed.

"Looked that way earlier," she mutters, but I speak before Sawyer can, pointing between Harlow and Ezra.

"Are you two still together?" I ask.

"Wow, you have some explaining to do," Ezra says with a grin to Harlow.

"Yes, thank you. Can we focus on one thing at a time?" she says.

"Yeah. The priority is how absurd this whole plan is," I remind them.

"I don't need your permission, Nico."

"Good, because you won't get it," I say, my patience at an end.

"Dude, what's your problem?" Sawyer grumbles. "You're so worried about her, join us. Help her out."

Is that why I'm so annoyed? Because what I want more than anything is to be able to defend this amazing girl, but I don't have that choice. Knowing me puts her in more danger, and god forbid, if she makes it through to The Games, I may wind up fighting against her. How can I do that? I'm doing the right thing, distancing myself. I need to be strong to protect her and protect myself from blowback in the process. There's complete silence, but Harlow tries to cover it.

"You don't have to. You've already helped so much," she says. Her eyes are full of defeat, and I wish I could change that, but there's no way I can do what she's asking of me. Not without painting an even bigger target on her back. Stepping forward, I cup her cheek before I can stop myself, touching her just one last time.

"Know that if I could, I would," I whisper to her, "but I can't. I'm so sorry. I'm out." A frown mars her brow.

Dropping my hand, I grab my bag and head to the door. "I'll see you around. Good luck." I don't turn back as I walk away from their apartment, likely for the last time.

Chapter 31

Harlow

NICO GOES, LEAVING A heavy silence in the room. We all know more is going on there, but we have no clue what it is. He seemed so defeated, and all I want to do is help him. But how do you help someone who continually pushes you away? How has my life become so overwhelming these last few weeks?

Before, it was simple. Work, bar, train, study. No feelings to worry about, no unexpected changes. Now, something new seems to pop up every day. First, we have the huge leap to take a chance with Ezra, the ups and downs of telling Sawyer how I feel and now knowing he's not exclusive, and then Nico inserting himself further into my life while holding back more than ever. For a heartless commitment-phobe, this is enough to send me to bed. So that's what I do. With a murmured excuse to the guys, I retreat to my room to curl up and try to relieve my headache. An hour later, I'm still stewing.

There's a light knock, and Sawyer pokes his head around the door. Despite my mood, the corners of my lips turn up. I will always be happy to see Sawyer. He sits in front of me on the bed before twisting to face me. "You wanna explain what's going on?" he asks.

"Which part?"

"Our part," he says, brushing some hair away from my face. "That will always be the most important part to me, that we're okay."

"We are okay," I whisper.

"But you're overwhelmed and would rather have space than let me help because you're mad at me, and I don't know why. Did I do something wrong? Did I make a mistake telling you how I feel? This is what I wanted to avoid. I want you to always be able to come to me."

He looks so lost that it makes me want to be brave, but not right now. I'm not ready yet. I want to pretend everything is fine for just a little longer, in case he can't commit to being with only me. I've only just got this, I'm not ready to give it up yet.

"Can we not fix the world right now?" I say. "Can we just leave that for a little bit?" He searches my eyes for a minute, and clearly decides I'm not falling off the edge just yet, because he smiles, albeit sadly.

"Whatever you want, Angel. And as much as I'd like to keep you here for myself, I think Ezra is waiting to talk to you too."

I groan and flop back on the bed. "Does he hate me for keeping this from him?"

"Why are you always so hard on yourself? He adores you."

"Okay," I say, sitting up and rolling my shoulders. "I'm ready." He leans forward and kisses me softly again.

"You're not going to war. Relax."

"It's scarier, right?" I say to him. "When it's not just sex? When there's feelings involved?" It's not just me who has a freak-out over every feeling, right?

"Yeah, it is. But it's also so much better. Just let your walls down for a little bit. It's worth it."

"Promise?"

"I promise." Then he stands up and leaves, and Ezra takes his place almost immediately.

"Hey," he says softly, and I smile back.

"Hey. I'm—"

"Do not say you're sorry. You were right. You don't owe me your secrets so soon after we've just met and started dating. But I hope you would have told me eventually."

"I get why you freaked," I concede. "This is going to be interesting, huh?"

"*Interesting* is one word for it. But if we're going to do this, then there's no one else I'd rather figure it out with."

"I'm going to make mistakes," I say to him. "I'm going to freak out and not know what to do, but I'm also going to be sorry when it happens."

"And I'll be here the whole way through," he reassures me.

"Yeah? Because you're the one who convinced me to give feelings a go. I'm blaming you if all this goes wrong." He laughs.

"Shoot your shot," he says with a grin.

I wake up in the morning feeling like I've slept forever, feeling the comforting warmth of Ezra against my back. I know it's ridiculous, but I'd missed him, and last night was great. There's a soft knock on the door, and Sawyer peeks his head round. I grin at him to show him it's okay to come in, and when he brings coffee, I think I get hearts in my eyes. He's in only sweats, hair still damp from a shower, and his muscles ripple as he bends to put the mug on the side. He looks utterly and divinely edible. Catching me checking him out, he raises a brow, and I lift the duvet in front of me to invite him in. Yes, I may have some issues with how this is working out, but we'll let my libido take charge for now. Enjoy the good times while they last. The serious conversations can wait for later.

He lays on his side facing me, twirling a loose bit of hair around his finger.

"Morning, Angel," he says softly. I glance back to check if Ezra has stirred, but his hand still rests heavy on my hip.

"Morning," I reply, trying to wriggle forward for a kiss, but Ezra's hold tightens, pulling my body further against his.

"Where are you going?" he asks playfully, voice deep with sleep.

"Stop being greedy, Ezra," Sawyer mocks as he closes the space between us instead. My skin prickles as I become aware of the position I'm in—naked and sandwiched between two of the hottest guys who, for the moment, are both mine. *Holy hell.*

"I'll always be greedy for Harlow," Ezra says into my hair. He lifts my knee and places it so it's over Sawyer's legs as Sawyer lifts the duvet and ducks his head, taking my nipple into his mouth. "Don't think I didn't notice those territorial markings," Ezra huffs as Sawyer grins against my breast, although, if anything, it seems to have made Ezra more turned on to see what Sawyer had left on me. Maybe inspired to leave more marks of his own. And with Sawyer encouraging me to send the photo, I think this multiple partner thing is going to be a lot of fun.

Ezra runs a hand down my ribs, over my waist and hips, before squeezing my ass roughly. I arch my back, pressing back into Ezra and forward in Sawyer, knowing I need more than this teasing. Ezra kisses the side of my neck, and if either of them care about how close they are, they don't say anything. Ezra's hand creeps down to cup me from behind before sinking a lone finger into my heat. My hips begin rocking of their own accord, desperate for more, when Sawyer adds a finger right in with Ezra's, and I nearly combust. They both slow as I quiver around them, backing me away from the edge, and I manage to suck in a breath.

"What, are you both psychic now?" I ask. I can *feel* their amusement.

"No, but we both know what you like." How they can know that already, I don't know, and I go to say exactly that, but their hands start moving and they speed up, and all thoughts leave my mind as they both fuck me with their hands. Sawyer continues weaving magic with his mouth in the front, and Ezra presses against me from behind, not entering but I can feel his hardness against my rear, and I'm so damn close. A hard bite from Ezra to the side of my neck tips me over, and I explode, moaning unintelligible words as I writhe and they carry me through it.

"Fuck, you're so beautiful," Sawyer breathes before I even open my eyes, and his lips press to mine.

"Okay, my turn to watch you come," Ezra declares, rolling my near-limp body over and pulling me down the bed with him. "How about we repeat that little performance with better equipment?" Does he mean . . . what does he mean?

My thighs tense just thinking about it, and even though I came less than a minute ago, a new urge starts to build. These guys make me insatiable.

He spins me and pulls a leg over his hips as I roll over to straddle him. He hugs me, and I kiss him for the first time this morning. I feel a hand lace into my hair as Ezra lets me go, and Sawyer pulls me back gently so I'm sitting over Ezra's lap, my back against Sawyer's front, with my head turned to see Sawyer and his molten eyes. Have they ever looked so dark?

"Keep your eyes on me," he demands, and I do, even as Ezra lifts my hips and then lowers them again as he pushes up into me. "Jesus Christ," Sawyer groans as my mouth pops open on a moan.

Ezra grips my hips tighter as he thrusts, and as Sawyer lets my hair go around my shoulders, I turn to see Ezra's eyes glued to the spot where we're joined.

"Lean forward, Angel." I clench around Ezra at what Sawyer's words mean, and he groans. I turn my head to the side to flick my hair over my shoulder before I do—and catch a glimpse of someone else in the mirror. It's so sudden and unexpected that I scream and throw myself to the bed, attempting to cover myself with the duvet.

Sawyer is out the door immediately, and when I hear a thump, I throw a discarded T-shirt and shorts on to go after him. He has Eli up against the wall with his forearm over his chest. Thank god he hadn't taken his sweats off yet.

"What the fuck are you doing?" he yells in his face, pressing him harder into the wall.

"Nothing," Eli says quickly. "Sorry! I was just looking for Ezra."

Ezra steps out of the bedroom, now wearing underwear, but he pauses behind the wall, a confused expression on his face. He hangs back where Eli can't see him, letting Sawyer take the lead.

"And peeking at the show?" Sawyer spits. "Getting an eyeful of our girl?" I've never seen Sawyer so angry or looking so dangerous.

"No, I'm sorry! It was an accident, I swear. I only saw her as she saw me."

He looks genuinely scared and apologetic, and he is my boyfriend's family, so I gently grab Sawyer's elbow.

"Sawyer, it's fine. It was a mistake. We should learn to lock the door," I joke. He doesn't react for a long moment, but finally, he releases him and stalks back to the bedroom. As soon as he's out of earshot, Eli's demeanor changes, and he looks me up and down with a leer that screws his whole face up.

"Seems you like being shared around, gorgeous. What's one more pair of eyes?" I'm so shocked I can't even respond. Unfortunately for him, Ezra hasn't left with Sawyer, and quicker than I can comprehend, he's in front of him and throwing a fist into his face. Blood spurts from Eli's nose as the force makes him bounce off the wall and to the ground. Ezra has a hand around his throat before he's even rolled.

"What the fuck did you just say?" he asks him, his voice deathly calm.

"Shit, I'm sorry! I shouldn't have."

"Not to me."

"Sorry, Harlow!" I nod numbly. I have no idea what's going to happen between them now. I don't want me to be the reason they fall out, and I feel responsible somehow, like I wound him up with my mistakes.

"Now get the fuck out and don't come in here unless you're invited. If I hear you say anything like that to her again, we're gonna have problems. Brothers or not."

Eli nods violently and scrambles up to leave as soon as Ezra releases his hand.

"You okay?" he asks me once he's shut and locked the door behind him.

"Yeah, I'm fine." I feel dirty and shocked and kind of scared, but I don't voice that bit. Ezra didn't see the look of pure evil on Eli's face. There's no doubt in my mind that if he had the opportunity to, he would hurt me, and I have no idea why. "I'm gonna go shower."

I scrub myself until my skin is sore. Even without touching me, I feel like his gaze is imprinted on me. Such a private and vulnerable moment, not meant for anyone else to witness, violated. When I get out, Sawyer is still furious. Even more so, and it dawns on me.

"You told him?" I say to Ezra.

"Yeah. Why wouldn't I?" he asks.

"He's still your family. He doesn't need you both to hate him." I don't want Ezra to have to choose. Who chooses a girl they met weeks ago over their own flesh and blood?

"He needs to keep his thoughts about you to himself." I can see they're too angry to reason with right now, so I nod and walk to my room.

Chapter 32

Ezra

Harlow waits for me in the lobby of the gym, looking incredible as always in her gym gear. Leaning down to give her a kiss, I ignore the glances and glares from every man in there as I grin down at *my* girl.

"I missed you," I say.

"You've got me." If those aren't the perfect words to hear.

We head into the room where Sawyer is finishing up with his previous client. While he walks toward us, Harlow strips off her overshirt, wraps her arms around his neck, and pulls him down for a passionate kiss. I don't know if she's staking her claim or she just really missed him, but either way, possessive Harlow is hot as fuck. Sawyer kisses her back like he quite likes it too. With a glare, the woman leaves.

"Fuck. Are we training, or do I need to lock the door?" I direct at Sawyer.

"Training. There's cameras in here," Sawyer says, taking a step back from Harlow and discreetly rearranging himself. Shame.

We're working on some close-combat self-defense, which is mainly grappling and learning ways to get out of holds. It's basically for Harlow to learn how to use the opponent's strength and size against them, as she probably won't get grabbed by anyone smaller than her. I'm watching Sawyer and joining in, because I'll practice with Harlow too, but also so he can teach me some hand-to-hand combat maneuvers. After what happened to Nico, it can't hurt.

Today, though, Harlow keeps faltering. She seems to know the moves, but it's like she forgets them halfway through. It takes me longer than it should to realize that Sawyer is teasing her. Every time he grabs her, he's brushing over her nipples. Every time she's pinned, his hand trails up her inner thigh. And each subtle caress makes that sexy blush more prominent over her chest.

She's taken to the mat again, and he flexes his hips, her mouth parting on a near silent gasp as she feels him against her. Her reflexes start to become jerky, like she's not focusing, but then they become slow and languid. She's not trying to win—she's content being wound up as she naturally melts into him. It's like a game of cat and mouse, and it's the hottest thing I've ever seen. I'm not even sure who's winning. They both seem to be getting what they want. I could watch it for hours, my dick sitting solid in my shorts.

They get into a tussle on the ground and Harlow starts to crawl away, but he easily grabs her thigh, flips her onto her back, and holds her legs against his chest. Then, quick as lightning, he bares her ass and plunges into her slit. He grinds once, twice, then pulls out and puts their clothing back to rights. If I wasn't watching them both so intently, I'd have missed the whole thing, and there's no way the camera will be able to see anything due to the angle. She lays there for a few seconds, mouth open as she blinks slowly at Sawyer's smug-as-fuck face before she lets him pull her to her feet. He then spins her to face the clock on the wall.

"My class will be here in a second," he says, "and there's no way on this earth they're going to see you come." She shivers in his arms, and he kisses the back of her neck, right over her tattoo. Just as he pulls back, the first member walks in. Good timing. They join me over by the bench and I pull her into my arms.

"You're the sexiest woman in the world," I tell her truthfully. "And now, I get to take you home and relieve you of all that pent-up frustration." I smirk at Sawyer.

"Asshole," he says good-naturedly.

On the way home, Harlow is quiet, and I wonder what's caused the change in mood.

"You okay?" I ask.

"Yeah," she says distractedly before pulling her bottom lip between her teeth. A sure sign she's worrying about something. I stop us in the street, free her lip, and cup her cheek.

"Talk to me," I say.

"What's the deal with sex between us?" she asks. "Like, with you and Sawyer? Are there rules?"

"Do you want there to be rules?" I ask.

"Not necessarily . . . but should I tell one of you if I'm going to have sex with the other one? Is that weird for you two?"

"Harlow, thinking of taking you while you're sated and pliable, all worked up by someone else, is the hottest thought," I say truthfully before laying a kiss to her shoulder. "Getting to make you come when someone else has brought you to the edge—the hottest thought." Another kiss to her neck. "Seeing where someone else has been, whether that's your swollen lips or their cum dripping out of you—*the hottest fucking thought*." She sways slightly, and I tighten my arms around her waist, pulling back so she's staring up at me with wide eyes and a parted mouth. I don't think I could've been any clearer. "You okay?" I ask.

"Yeah, but I think you should probably get me home and naked as soon as possible, okay?"

"Good, because I've been hard since you half-stripped for Sawyer, and I need to be inside you pronto."

I'm pressed into her from behind as she unlocks her door, kissing the exposed skin of her shoulder and stroking the underside of her breast through her crop top, desperate to shed some of these clothes.

"I still can't believe I get to do this," I murmur into her skin.

"You can do a lot more than that," she replies, pressing her ass against my crotch, and I groan.

"Hurry up!" I growl as she fumbles with the keys.

"You're distracting me," she laughs breathily. Just then, my front door opens on the other side of the hall, and Eli stands there.

"Hey, Harlow," he calls easily, as if I'm not getting ready to maul her right here and now.

"Hi," she calls awkwardly, peering around me.

"Have you got a second?" I know she won't say no, because she's too polite, so I don't let her decide.

"Give us an hour," I say to him as she finally gets the door open and I push her inside.

"An hour, huh?" she whispers as I slam the door behind me.

"Oh yeah. Territorial Harlow is sexy as fuck," I tell her, wrapping my arms around her waist.

"Yeah? Show me how sexy," she whispers.

"Anytime," I say. And in the meantime, I also have a certain photo to get back at Sawyer for.

Two hours later, Harlow rolls out of bed with considerable effort and a sigh.

"Where are you going?"

"I said I'd see Eli, remember."

I shrug. "He can wait." He can. She doesn't have to give him any of her time if she doesn't want to. Eli has never been a horrible person, and I was shocked when I heard how he spoke to Harlow before. He said he just got his guard up after his pride was dented by being manhandled by Sawyer, insisted he didn't do anything wrong and took it out on her, but that's not an excuse and he knows exactly how I feel about it.

"He's your brother," she says.

"So he'll be happy for me that I found someone I like so much that I can't let them leave this bed," I argue, and she doesn't protest, giggling as I pull her back under the covers.

Chapter 33

Harlow

I WAKE UP TO the featherlight touch of a kiss on my cheek. Instinctively, I turn my face and wind my arms around his neck, pulling him back for a proper kiss without opening my eyes. I feel the breadth of his shoulders and smell the scent of our shared shower gel. *Sawyer.* He groans when I run my nails in the back of his hair.

"I've got to go, Angel."

"Why?" I whine, just a tiny bit.

"I've got an early class. You get some more sleep. I'll see you later." He kisses me again quickly, and I settle back into bed as a warm hand lands on my waist and a chaste kiss drops onto the back of my shoulder. *Ezra.* I try to pull his arm around my waist and down, and he chuckles lightly.

"I'm just leaving," he says.

I sigh overdramatically.

"Two guys in my bed and not one to wake me up the proper way."

"And how is that?" Sawyer asks from the far side of the room.

"Full."

A pair of groans come from opposite sides of the space, and my lips tip up in a wry smile.

"We'll bear that in mind for next time," Ezra whispers before placing a kiss on my cheek, and then he's gone too.

I think I might be the happiest I've ever felt in my life. No, I'm sure I am. Ezra was right—my heart has expanded like a universe, enveloping both of my guys. I've still not been brave enough to speak to Sawyer about what I saw that day in the gym, but I don't want to rock the boat right now, not when everything's going so well. I also haven't seen Nico since he found out about The Games, and I feel like he's changed some shifts to avoid me, but he has a month left before he officially leaves, so surely he can't avoid me forever?

It's Liv's birthday tonight, and we've all been invited out for drinks to celebrate. The guys went over a little bit ago, and I've enjoyed having the space to get ready without the urge to jump one—or both—of them. No dressing would be happening otherwise. I've chosen a dusky pink dress that hugs every curve, the ruching accentuating the dip between my waist and hips and highlighting my legs. Pairing it with sky-high heels and my blond hair around my shoulders in waves, I'm leaning into the Barbie image tonight, but you know what? I'm not hating it. I'm owning it and using it as a positive rather than a negative, just like Ezra said. He's wise, that one.

Just as I'm getting ready to leave, Fleur calls me.

"Hey," I say brightly, but I stop frozen when I hear her sniffling. "Fleur, what's going on?"

"Harlow, can I come over?" she asks with a sob.

"Of course." Something's definitely wrong. I don't think she's ever called me in tears before—she's not an emotional person. Well, she wasn't, before Lee.

"Is there anyone there? I don't want anyone to see me," she says.

"No, it's just me." The bell buzzes then, and it's her already. I hang up and let her in, doing a double take at her tear-streaked face and immediately taking her into my arms.

"Fleur, what's going on?" Her eyes are puffy, and she looks knackered.

"Lee goes tomorrow," she sobs into my shoulder. Shit, I'm the worst. I've been in my happy little bubble while her heart is breaking.

"I'm so, so—"

"And I think I'm pregnant." Oh my god. *Oh my god.* I just hold her, letting her get it all out, until her tears dry and she's hiccuping. Eventually, I pull her back so I can get a look at her. "What am I going to do?" she asks.

"You're going to do a test," I say simply. She nods, seeming like she's in shock. I make her comfy and then duck to the small shop on the corner, praying they have pregnancy tests, and I blush as I pay for it in my party dress. I get home and usher Fleur into the bathroom, taking charge while she follows my instructions blankly. When she's finished, she sets the stick on the side, and we both turn away from it as I set a timer on my phone.

Just then, the front door opens and Fleur jumps, eyes wide and holding her hand over her mouth. I guess nobody knows she's here, and she likely doesn't want to see anyone in this state, which is understandable.

"Harlow?" Sawyer calls. "Everything okay?"

"Yeah, absolutely," I yell back through the bathroom door. "I just need a few more minutes."

"Okay, I'll wait for you," he says.

"No, it's fine," I say quickly, looking back at Fleur. "Go back to the party. I'll meet you there soon."

The next time he speaks, his voice sounds closer. "Are you sure everything's okay?" he asks through the bathroom door.

"Yep," I call back a little too brightly, but he must sense I need space, because he finally agrees to meet me back at Ezra's. We hear the door shut again and both sag in relief.

"Thank you so much for this. I didn't even ask if you were free," Fleur says.

"I'm always free for you," I reassure her. She smiles weakly at me.

"You look insane, by the way. You're worth the wait for Sawyer." I grin back at her in thanks, and she wrings her hands. "Jesus. I can't even have a drink to take the edge off. What if I am?"

"What are you hoping for?" I ask.

"Stupidly? Stupidly, I hope I am. It's what I've always wanted. But what will I do?"

"You'll take it and show Lee, and you'll work it out together. You know I'm always here for you, no matter what you decide. But he's a decent guy, and he deserves to know. You two are amazing together. *If* it's positive, you'll work it out as a team."

"You make it sound easy," she says with a small laugh.

"I'm pretty sure this is the easiest bit, so I hope so," I say. The blare of my phone alarm stops any more words, and she takes a deep breath before she spins and picks up the stick. She freezes.

"Well?!" I ask.

She turns it to face me, and my face splits into the biggest smile. "Congratulations! You're pregnant!" I hug her to me, holding the offending stick away from us as we laugh, hug, and cry all at the same time, and when I finally release her, she's still in shock. Taking the test off her, I hold it up in front of me, making sure not to touch the other end. I don't think I'll ever be *that* close to anyone.

"Why are you taking a picture?" she finally asks.

"Because when you've finally taken all of this in, I'll send it to you, and you can remember this moment and how much happiness is in it. I have a feeling you're not processing at the moment, but it'll come. It'll all be okay."

"You are the best," she replies simply. It reminds me of Sawyer and how I've said that to him for years, and I think of my guys waiting for me, of *my* happy ending. "Okay, I'm gonna tell him," she says. *Me too*, I think.

"Keep me updated?" I say.

"Of course. Thank you. I'm going to go, and I'm so sorry I messed up your plans!" she says, wiping the tears from her face.

"They're not messed up. I'm glad you came." I give her one last hug.

"Thanks, Harlow."

When Fleur has left and I've checked I look okay again, I join everyone over at Ezra's. Sawyer pounces on me as soon as I enter, checking my face for any signs of distress. I may have gotten a little teary at Fleur's news, but hopefully I'm not too red.

"I'm fine," I beam at him. "Just needed some extra time."

"Okay," he says, not completely convinced, but he plays it off. "The extra time was spent well. You look incredible." I don't get to reply before arms loop around my waist from behind.

"Fuck, you look amazing. My very own Barbie," Ezra growls into my ear, and I heat, looking up to let Sawyer see the lust that fills my eyes.

"Do we have to go out at all? We live right across the hall, we can just go home?" he asks, not looking away from me, which makes me smile and step away from them both.

"Yes, we do, we're here for Liv's birthday. Keep your hands to yourself," I tease as I go to find Liv.

It's not long before we head to the bar, where we have a great evening, laughing and drinking with Liv—who I love—and even Eli is being half-decent. Maybe it was a turning point with us and he'll be okay now?

Coming back from the toilet, I scan the crowd for one of my guys and freeze when I see the girl from Ezra's housewarming party. Standing way too close to Sawyer. Her hand is stroking his arm as she reaches on her tiptoes and whispers into his ear, her body pressed up against his. And he seems to be... letting her. I push my way through the crowd to find Ezra, but before I can, Sawyer is suddenly in front of me.

"Hey, there you are," he says.

"I'm surprised you realized I was gone," I snap back at him. He frowns down at me and my change in mood.

"Of course I did. What's wrong?"

"Nothing. I'm trying to find Ezra," I say. His brows lift this time.

"You want Ezra instead?" he asks.

"Just how you want the girl from the housewarming instead? Or the girl from the gym? I'm right here, Sawyer. I see you with them, and even if I know it's happening, it still hurts."

"What girl from the gym?" he asks.

"The one who had her hand around your dick." My phone vibrates in my hand, and I'm planning to ignore it until I see Fleur's name on the screen.

"Harlow—"

"I have to take this," I say, holding up my phone. I walk past him and to a quieter corner, where I put my finger in one ear and hold my phone up. "Hello?"

"Hey, have you got a minute?" Fleur asks. Her voice is fairly even, so that's a good sign. "I'm outside, just around the corner."

"One minute, I'll come to you," I say, I don't know why Fleur has come here to see me so desperately, but with her being so upset earlier, I need to find out. Leaving the party behind, I step outside the bar and see Fleur leaning against Lee's bonnet, slightly further down. I run over and hug her instinctively before I lean down to wave at him, and he waves back with a huge grin.

"He took it well, then?" I ask. Fleur's huge smile matches his.

"He did. We talked it all through, and I'm moving with him." My mouth drops, and she rushes to justify herself. "I know it's quick and it's probably really stupid, but—"

"It's not!" I interrupt her. "I think it's a great idea. It just shocked me that you're moving away from me. Like . . . now?" I ask.

"Now," she says with a teary smile. "I know, I know it's sudden, but it's not too far, not really." She winces. "We can still see each other! I'll text you the address soon."

"Speaking of texting . . ." I send her the photo from earlier before I forget. Her phone dings, and she beams when she sees what it is.

"Thank you so much, Harlow."

"Any time." I give her a tight squeeze, knowing this may be the last time I see my best friend for a while. "Call me when you get there?" I ask.

Fleur nods, and I hug her again before I watch her get in the car and drive off to her new future. Turning back to the bar, I know I made a mistake calling Sawyer out tonight, of all nights to do it. It's Liv's birthday, and I don't want to fight. I should've been brave enough to ask him about exclusivity sooner, but I didn't, and now I've sulked like a teenager and ruined his night too. Well, it's time to face the music and see what Sawyer actually thinks is going on here.

I take a deep breath and walk back into the bar, pushing through a big crowd of people at the entrance. They're all taller than me, and I feel like the crowd is never-ending. I'm lost in the throng of people when I feel strong arms around my waist. Hoping it's Sawyer and I can see if we can have an adult conversation about everything, I try to spin toward him. The crowd is packed too tight, though, and it's darker here, so I let him push me forward with his body sturdy at my back. He leads me into a corridor off to the side, and finally, we have some free space. Turning to face him, my brain is lagging, and by the time I register that someone who definitely isn't Sawyer has got me alone, there's a cold, solid object pressed against my side. *Fuck. How do I fight against a gun?*

"Don't make a sound," he whispers. Fear freezes the breath in my lungs, and I couldn't scream if I wanted to, although it doesn't seem like a great idea right now. I'm working on trying to suck in a breath and not completely freaking out, knowing that I need to be calm if I'm going to figure out how to get out of this, but I don't get that far before something covers my mouth and nose. He's trying to gag me?

There's suddenly way too many hands on my body, and the room starts to spin. Even though I'm vigorously trying to shake my head free, slowly at first and then all at once, everything goes black.

To be continued in We Will Conquer, book two of The Games Trilogy...

ALSO BY GENEVIEVE JASPER

THE ELITE AT OAKVIEW U SERIES
When We're Alone

All my life I've been told "be seen but not heard," and I'm suffocating. Going through the motions to survive until I get my chance, my shot to prove I'm just as valuable as any man that my Dad wants me to snare.

When my father dies unexpectedly, I'm free—until I'm not. With our finances and the business under another man's control, we're forced to move in with Dad's business partner and his son, Stone. He hates me, and I don't know why, but I won't take it lying down.

I just want to get through my last year of university unscathed. When Stone and the rest of the Elite continue to target me, I have no choice. The fighter comes out. They have no idea what I survived at the hands of my father. They won't break me.

When We're Alone is a contemporary romance novel suitable only for readers 18+ due to language and sexual scenes. This is an enemies to lovers standalone book with characters of university age. This book contains mature themes such as bullying and death, but our main characters will get their happily ever after (or for now). A full list of trigger warnings can be found at the front of the book.

IRONHAVEN SERIES
Her Titans

I'm finally single again and am ready for my wild phase. Enter Atlas, the Viking God in a three-piece suit. I think it's a one-night stand; simple, no-strings fun, right? Now he wants me to be his girl. But can I really be his when I've also developed feelings for his two best friends? Together, they are the Titans – business flippers rumoured to have a big presence in the criminal underground, and they are used to sharing. Do I follow my head, or my heart? Do I even have a choice?

When my house burns down, I discover someone is trying to warn the Titans away from me and claim me as theirs. Everyone in Ironhaven has secrets, and I didn't even know about my own. Can the Titans find my stalker before it's too late? I only wanted a wild phase, but it may wind up being the ride of my life.

Her Titans is a contemporary reverse harem romance novel, suitable only for readers 18+ due to language and sexual scenes. Whilst the main characters in Her Titans get their Happily Ever After in this book, there will be other unanswered questions to be addressed later in the series. Her Titans contains references to gangs and violence and contains themes such as kidnapping, stalking, and grievous bodily assault.

Her Vipers

After 3 years in prison for a crime I didn't commit, I'm looking forward to getting my life back on track. That is, until I find out my 'accidental' incarceration wasn't so accidental after all. Somebody murdered my father and framed me. The only clue I have to find out who's behind it all is the Vipers Motorcycle Club, and the three legacies set to take over the throne. Caus, Echis and Kofi swear they had nothing to do with me being framed, and they want answers too.

When I find myself working in their bar and sleeping in their beds, I know I'll need to protect my heart and have my own back. They may say they are on my side, but the Vipers screwed me over once before. What's to say it won't happen again? I don't need them. I can figure out the secrets of my past and get revenge just fine on my own. They may know my twin sister, but they don't know me.

Her Vipers is a contemporary reverse harem romance novel, suitable only for readers 18+ due to language and sexual scenes. Whilst the main characters in Her Vipers get their Happily Ever After in this book, there may be unresolved issues to be addressed in the final book of the series. Her Vipers contains references to gangs and violence and contains themes such as kidnapping, murder, prison, and grievous bodily assault.

Her Sentries

While my best friends each found love with gang leaders, my life spiralled out of control. Threats, secrets, even kidnappings. Ironhaven doesn't feel safe anymore.

I was forced to retreat, but now I'm ready to take my life back, starting with returning to Ironhaven. But moving on isn't as easy as I hoped. I develop feelings for not one, but three men.

Jeremy, who wants to protect me but nothing more.

Abel, the charming, sweet and funny guy who is just the distraction I need.

And Jackson, the asshole detective looking to bring those close to me down.

But the heart wants what the heart wants—and my heart is telling me there's more to him than it seems.

I want my happily ever after but it seems out of reach. With my heart belonging to three different men, how can I choose between them? And when I'm caught in the crosshairs of someone else's vendetta, who will save me?

Her Sentries is a contemporary reverse harem romance novel, suitable only for readers 18+ due to language and sexual scenes. This is the final book in the Ironhaven series and will have a happy ending. Her Sentries references gangs and violence, and contains themes such as murder, stalking, and grievous bodily assault.

ABOUT THE AUTHOR

GENEVIEVE JASPER IS A British romance author who loves angst, protective alphas, and *all* the spice. She adores reading just as much as writing and prefers to do both while cuddled on the sofa with her pooch.

You can find Genevieve on Facebook, Instagram, and Tik Tok.

Printed in Great Britain
by Amazon